CW00584871

TORMENTED

PATRICIA A SUTCLIFFE

ISBN:9798642455326

All characters and events in this

publication are fictitious and any resemblance

to real persons living or dead is

purely coincidental.

DEDICATION

This book is dedicated to my grandchildren

LUCAS and OLIVIA

ACKNOWLEDGMENTS

John for his excellent editing skills

Adam, Nikki, Richard and Alice

for their encouragement and feedback

TORMENTED

ANGEL BOYLE

Angel spat on her finger. She rubbed hard at the congealed blood splattered across her wrist. Annoyed. If it was hers, she had been careless, and that was an enormous mistake. She had planned well but had allowed herself to become overwhelmed, her need for vengeance great. Such sloppiness she dares not tolerate. It must not happen again.

She pinched herself hard, twisting the flesh between thumb and forefinger. Pain surged through her body. It gave her an immediate release. It was enough to change the physical assault to a verbal assault. 'Idiot, fool, what the fuck were you thinking?' Her anger vented, she shifted her focus, pressed the red button on the washing machine and smiled as it drummed into life. Another hour, it would remove all evidence.

An exhilarated Angel took several breaths, drawing in the air through her nostrils and releasing out through the mouth. A common practice she used to settle her mind. It was now time to concentrate on her latest book.

'Think, stupid girl'. Angel muttered as she struggled to put pen to paper, her mind fixated on things other than writing children's books. The craft she once loved no longer came easily to her. It had now become a necessity, affording her the finance and cover she needed to fulfil her mission.

Angel craved isolation; As an author, she could write in solitude. Get lost in her own creative mind. This was the perfect profession for her.

When sleep eluded her, she worked long hours into the night. It was her private time, a time to become immersed in her own thoughts. Thoughts that drifted from magical, fairy-tale worlds, to dark, tormented places, deep within her psyche.

Angel Boyle lived a life of stark contrast. A world clouded by confusion and conflict, invented to punish the guilty and reward justice. A life that was not ordinary.

As a writer, she had a unique ability to transport herself back with the flick of a switch. This allowed her to bond with her young audiences and played an enormous part in her success.

Angel thrived on the recall of vivid childhood stories, Hans Christian Andersen, Grimm's Fairy Tales, stories she adored so much. She loved to close her eyes and relive them, word for word, her mother's voice, the narrator, in her ear. This brought great comfort. She sensed her presence, her warmth. The sweet aroma of lavender in the air. It made her safe. It told her everything was okay.

Angel needed to sense her mother around her. A need that grew stronger with each passing day, overtaking her ambitions as a writer. A pleasure that was now dead to her, rotting in the grave with her mother.

In frustration, she threw the pen at the wall with a crack. It fell lifeless to the floor. It would write no more today. Tears rolled from Angel's eyes. She twisted her long red hair around her index finger, she pulled hard on the roots causing just enough pain to bring her back to her reality.

Tonight's walk had stirred up Angel's senses, making her restless but satisfied. She tucked her long shapely legs beneath her, nestling against the large snuggle cushion that adorned her favourite chair. She reached over the side, pressed a button, the leg rest sprang outwards. Tomorrow, another day.

Angel met with an empty gym, for which she was thankful. Any anger released into her workout. A short time later she was on her way home again, back to the crisp, clean apartment, the sanctuary she loved.

The Mews Penthouse apartment was somewhere private, out of the public eye, finding it had ended her search. A prime but secluded position overlooking

Midway Park on the edge of Town. Chosen for its location, cost, exclusivity, the place only successful people afforded to live in. No one from her past, or present, bothered her here. Her mother would be proud. That mattered, mattered so much.

Godliness is next to cleanliness' Carrie's words echoed around the daily strict cleaning regime in the Penthouse. It was one of her mother's favourite, often repeated phrases. One muttered by Angel every time she opened the cleaning closet door.

Angel Boyle was a success. She had money, owned her own upmarket apartment, the result of several much-read children's books., Angel enjoyed the finer things in life, it meant nothing to her. She had secrets, tragic secrets living deep within her, never leaving her thoughts.

Angel had achieved everything a mother would wish for her child; Carrie would have been proud, but Carrie wasn't here to share in Angel's success. Carrie was dead. Taken without warning, without justice, the result of a heinous crime. A crime that Angel Boyle did not forget or forgive. A crime that resounded in the black visions of her nightmares, waking her in terror, saturating her living thoughts.

The only child of Carrie and Eddie Boyle, Angel had the looks and mannerisms that had drawn her father to her mother many years before. Amazonian in stature, at 5'9" tall, she was muscular and fit. A physique gained through the pain of gruelling daily workouts during which she had developed a strength envied by many an ardent gym enthusiast. To her, it was of no importance.

In an emergency Angel Boyle could look after herself. That was of importance. She had to be she knew it. Her overriding need to protect herself at all costs was an obsession, a driving force that pushed her to the limits in all she did.

Singular in mind, she had, by choice, no close friends. Her only living relative, her father, whom she saw but for whom she had no great love. Her feelings for him were cold, the way she looked at him, accusing, the information he provided her with, needed.

She leant back, her head on the couch. She slid her tongue over her full lips, twitching her nose as she did so: she was, without doubt, a stunner. Angel had looks that would attract anyone she set her sights on, but boyfriends were now a thing of the past for her. Normality, she would never have again.

Aware of the television droning on in the background, she closed her eyes. She needed to spend time with her mother. it had become a ritual. it prepared her mind to walk the gloomy streets she once loved to play in as a child. Now she saw them for what they were, neglected. Darkly lit back alleys that grew dirtier and uglier with each passing year.

She sank deeper, gave a slight smile and breathed deeply, recalling the scent of her mother's perfume. The memory embedded deep into her senses brought Carrie back to her side. A child again. She remembered the soft hair brushing her cheek. The way her mother leant to kiss her goodnight. Here she was safe.

A tear ran down her cheek. She struggled to hold the vision. It was no good. the scene turned into a darker, uglier one. It transported angel to another place. A dark place full of torment'. Time heals' they said. It doesn't.

With little moonlight, it was getting dark outside. Time for Angel's nightly regime to begin. She scanned the darkness, her eyes focussed on the park. She then pulled the blind and closed out the remaining light to become engulfed in the privacy of her own world. A privacy she always protected. A privacy she took substantial lengths to protect. Heavy brocade curtains completed the blackout.

Angel stroked the ornate mantel clock, the last gift from her mother. She took in the time. 7.13pm? It would be awhile yet before she got ready. Started her lengthy, methodical preparation.

Aware of the risk of walking out late at night, she had trained herself well to be alert to her surroundings. Readiness was key to remaining safe. Nasty surprises would not catch her out. Of this, she was sure.

TORMENTED

The red satin dress clung to her body; its low revealing neckline showed off her shapely body. She tied her waist length hair into bunches and let it hang across her shoulders, before scooping it into a bun and pulling on the shoulder length brown wig. She looked much younger than her 31 years.

Next, she rubbed a thick layer of pan stick into her face, Applied the bright red lipstick and smacked her lips together. The look completed with dark blue eye shadow, false lashes and green contact lens. Looking every inch, a tart. She fastened the straps of black high-heeled shoes. Pulled on her short, white fur coat, picked up her gloves, checked the contents of her red patent shoulder bag and headed for the door.

She took a deep breath. She wouldn't need to stop out longer than necessary. Angel walked in the park's direction, the brightness of her coat standing out against the poorly lit streetlight. A shiver ran through her. It was now 9.50 pm: The smack heads would gather, hoping to score. She accepted them, they accepted her, she didn't fear them.

The gravel on the path crunched, heels clicking, as she hurried. Her head moving around, the shadows of the trees lining her way played games with her mind. 'Want some love?' The bandstand, where the dealers lurked in the darkness, loomed up in front of her. Angle pushed a crisp £10 note into a waiting, grasping hand.

She grabbed the small, white packet and thrust it into her bag. She would need this later.

As she entered the precinct, Angel observed the drinkers milling in and out of the Town's bars. She continued: Her destination pre-determined. A string of lewd comments followed her. She reached Baker Street. Took out a second pair of gloves, thicker than the black nylon ones she was already wearing, tugged them on, stretching out her fingers. It was important that they fit snuggly.

At the bottom of the Baker Street stood the Half Moon Public House. This area of Town, older than the rest, still boasted cobbled sidewalks, unsuited to modern shoes. The black oak door faced her, she pushed it open, walked into the bar and back into time. Gas lamps still hung from heavy wooden rafters, a Memento to the past. Now lit by electricity, the interior's visibility was still poor, thanks in part to the ominous nicotine stains clinging to the ceiling.

Angel looked hard at the red flock wallpaper and embroidered seating surrounded the walls. Aware of the looks from its regulars, the disdain on the women's faces and lusting eyes of the men, she picked up the pint of cider, took a long sip, placed it back on the bar, turned on her heels and with a sway of her hips, left. She knew no one would recognise her as Eddie's red haired, blue eyed, daughter. They didn't.

TORMENTED

Sparse moonlight and few stars enabled Angel to stand half hidden under the cover of the pub's smoking canopy. Held a finger to her left nostril, drew on the white powder, repeating the same action with her right nostril. Now she was ready. The high was almost instantaneous; the cocaine absorbed through her nasal tissues, entering her bloodstream and her brain. Once there, interfering with her emotions causing her to become euphoric.

A heightened, exaggerated sense of excitement flowed over her. She was alert, energy surging through her veins, strong and fearless. Experience told her the effect would be short lived, timing was now essential. She needed to work quickly and get back to her apartment.

Baker Street was the ideal location. Back streets led off all along its length, forming networks of dark, secluded ginnels. A haven for the Town's petty criminals. A place Eddie Boyle often reported on.

Swaying, alert, eyes wide, she noticed footsteps behind her. A cracked, gravelly voice broke the silence. 'Hey love, want some company?' Angel's mouth tightened. 'Hey, you wait up. I'll walk you home,' the drunk slurred his words.

She slowed her pace, allowing the stranger to come up alongside her. A thick, stubby arm slid around her shoulder. The stench of stale alcohol drifted into her nostrils, mingled with cigarette smoke.

The stranger swayed, stumbled and grabbed at her coat. Beer befuddling his brain. Angel held his weight with her arm. 'What's up with you then, can't you speak?' She remained silent. They levelled with the ginnel. She steered him towards it. He snorted. 'More fucking like it.'

Well-lit by the streetlamp at its entrance, the alleyway descended into darkness as they half walked, half stumbled, further along it. Eager to get down to business, the rotund bellied man attempted to round on Angel, stopping her in her tracks. 'How much then?' his voice aggressive. Still she didn't speak but continued to push him further into the alley.

A glimmer of light emanated from the lamp at the far end. Agitated, he tried to swing her round. Angel stopped to face him, her back up against the cold of the brick wall, the heel of her shoe slipping in the gutter that ran the full length of the alleyway.

The place was perfect, Angel smiled. She glanced at her watch. 10.14pm, still early. Another 30 minutes before the regulars of the Moon would stagger out.

Her pupils wide, she looked into his pig-like, squinty eyes. The veins in his neck were standing out. He was getting excited, fumbling with his zipper. He rubbed

Angel's right breast, his face becoming red and bloated. Sweat stood out on his forehead in droplets.

He pressed his body against hers to pin her to the wall. She positioned her knee between his thighs. Annoyed, he tried to force her head downwards towards his crotch area. 'Come on tart, stop fucking about.' Panting, he continued his tirade. 'Dirty bag, just a dirty bag, asking for it.' Eager to finish, to get back to his cosy family home, his unsuspecting wife, he slapped Angel hard.

The flow of abuse now thick and fast, vicious and angry. Angel turned, her face smarting, the stench of his foul breath making her sick. He struggled to push her knee away. Tried to control her movements. She reached for the bag lying by her left foot. 'Talk dirty to me, fucking bitch. Do you hear me talk dirty, I said................................'?

The thud came with tremendous force. The stranger's eyes opened wide in disbelief; his words deadened by the impact. He held a shaking hand to his chest, gasped, fighting for breath. Blood bubbled and ran through his stubby fingers. Angel waited until the weight went still. The heavy carcass fell away from her, it slid to the ground with a dull thump. Adrenaline surging, she picked up her bag, took out a thin plastic box, folded brown carrier bag, black pack, a mac, flat shoes, a packet of baby wipes and set to work.

As they stumbled back to their families, the revellers paid little more than a fleeting glance to the ominous figure clad in a black mac. They were far too drunk to notice anything but the pavement in front of them.

Once in the park, Angel hurried, moving stealthily beneath the shadows of the trees. This was a path she knew well, memorising it many times during her daily walks. Routine was important. Mastering it gave her a sense of satisfaction. Moments later, she slipped unseen into her apartment block.

TORMENTED

Eddie Boyle

A bony arm reached outward. He struggled to swipe the old clock to the floor. He cursed as his arm banged hard on the grimy bedside table, recoiling in pain as he launched a soiled pillow. The damp missile, marked from the blood-stained spittle, hit its mark, silencing the cold, barren room.

Eddie Boyle had woken to the odour of soiled bedding drifting into his nostrils. Familiar stiffness in his aching limbs curled back into a foetal position and slumped back into the mattress. He battled his thoughts. He tried to relate to the present time, pulling a pillow across his head to drive out the buzzing. It was of no use. Determined, it pierced through the silence of his darkened mind, echoing and resounding, drilling at his very being.

A shaking hand moved towards his head. The familiar pounding told him it had been a good session. His eyes sore from rubbing. Irritated him. He tried to focus on the one remaining photo of Carrie. Her eyes appeared fixated on him, smiling. Pain rushed through his thoughts. He averted his gaze.

Tatty curtains, strung across a sash framed window, allowed only a glint of sunlight to stream into the dimly lit interior. It was still early. Eddie's spindly legs fought to release themselves from tangled, ragged blankets. He winced at the sharp pain in his lower back. Another fall, he vaguely remembered. Everything else remained a blank.

Eddie Boyle looked crushed, beaten down by the events of the past years. He had fought but failed to control his life. Now, on the verge of giving up, he had lost hope.

A broken drawer in the bedside cabinet coughed up a packet of ibuprofen. He picked up a cracked glass of tepid water, threw his head back and, in a single gulp, downed a handful of tablets.

Disgusted, Eddie prodded at his sallow face, grimacing at his gaunt frame. He threw on a grey vest, too short for his body. He shook. 'Carrie' There was no reply. She was gone, gone forever, and with her, his soul. His once coherent memories now becoming muddied and distorted.

Through the cracked mirror stared empty pale blue eyes, tinged yellow, heavy and sunken. His weathered face bore the remnants of a black eye, evidence of another fight he wouldn't remember.

Fingers, arthritic and crooked, poked at the lines etched in his face. He stared at his balding hair line. Once a mop of thick blonde waves, now sparse and greasy. Narrow, pale lips parted, revealing gap filled, stained teeth, grinning mechanically. Eddie Boyle, ashamed at the state he had allowed himself to get into, lacked the willpower to change the brief life he had remaining.

With a lurch he reached forward, grabbing at the half empty whisky bottle. He took a long swig, sighed and savoured the amber liquid. It tasted good, warming his dry throat as it slid down his gullet. The fuzziness that was on his mind now beginning to subside. Refreshed, Eddie heaved his tired body up and urinated into the cracked pot sink, grabbed his dark green flannel and began washing himself down.

Done, he pulled the makeshift handle of the wardrobe door. A fusty odour escaped into the room. He took out a creased checked shirt.

Eddie drew on a cigarette, its nectar bitter but satisfying. Still remembered by some as an honest, award-winning reporter and more out of compassion and pity than genuine need, he had retained his job on the local Castleton Gazette. Not that anything worth reporting ever happened in the small industrial town of

Castleton but, if it did, it was known that Eddie Boyle, drunkard or not, would be the first to hear about it.

Aware of tragedy behind the death of Carrie, Police officers remained supportive of Eddie. Officers like Bobby Brooks, a no nonsense, much respected police inspector who held a special allegiance towards him. When sober, it was to Bobby's desk that Eddie went for inside information, the pair often sharing a pint in the Half Moon.

Eddie, a regular in the Half Moon for longer than his memory serves, frequented it most nights. Here he reminisced about his evenings spent with Carrie. Dart matches, cracking the dominoes, beating all opposition. Eddie Boyle had been a star player in the Moon's league topping Darts and Dominoes team. Never missing a match, never letting the team down. Carrie, his long-suffering, accommodating wife, always by his side.

Built in early Victorian times, The Moon, as it was fondly known to the locals., was as Victorian on the inside as it was on the outside. It had kept most of its original features. The interior was grim, reeked of age and had an odour that clung in the air. A large open fire crackled a welcome, keeping its regular warmth on chilly winter nights. The wooden mantlepiece, boasting a pair of compulsory pot dogs, topped a tiled hearth, a scuttle filled with logs, coal now long gone along with the closure of the pits, a reminder of the Town's industrial past. A crooked poker rested on a small, well-worn hand brush and dustpan lying near the fire grate.

The aged, mahogany horseshoe bar stood as the Moon's centrepiece propping up the locals as it had done Eddie on many a boozy night. It did the same out of necessity now, the lively chatter he had so engaged in before, now sparse and stunted.

The snug where Carrie sat, exchanging local gossip with the abandoned woman of the darts and dominoes team, their haven. Decorated in the same thick dark cream anaglypta that covered the rest of the pub's walls. Painted so many times over the years, its diamond pattern had become raised in thick ridges. To be outdone only by the sticky, threadbare carpets.

Bobby Brooks, like Eddie, was in his mid-50's. They had grown up together, attended the same schools, fought together, started their careers becoming firm friends along the way.

Only when Eddie moved South, attracted by one of the big Nationals, were they separated. Bobby, filled with admiration as his friend, became a well-known, much-admired crime reporter.

Bobby, less ambitious, had never been outside of Castleton. Instead of choosing to serve the community he loved. His working life spent in the small police station. Smelling of polish and lavender. Success had not eluded him, however, since achieving the post of Inspector early in his career. A post he remained in, a post which allowed him to stay a hand's on 'good' copper. The role he relished along with the two lapel pips fastened on his collar.

Six foot in stocking feet, Bobby Brooks had a 'Don't fuck with me' look. He arrived on the scene to find Carrie Boyle's lifeless body on the floor of her bedroom, cut down from the rafters by Eddie. Everything else in the home remained the same. Bobby had grimaced at the black swollen, contorted face, eyes rolled back, tongue lolled to the side.

With absolute remorse, he had pinned a screaming Eddie down. The situation surreal as he watched Carrie's twisted frame being picked over by forensics. Prodded by the coroner, taken out and loaded unceremoniously into a body bag. This was one suicide that Eddie Boyle would not report on.

The pure horror of the incident left Eddie Boyle unrecognisable. Gone the smartly dressed, dapper reporter whose second home was Fleet Street. Gone the many awards his skills as a journalist gained him, gone along, ripped from him with his zest for life or for living.

Prior to Carrie's untimely death, everyone recognised Eddie Boyle as having a nose for a good story. He was the darling of the press, always there on the front line in the cutthroat world of journalism.

Fed up with the mundane 9 to 5 salesman role they had pushed him into from school, he gambled on a new career, putting study before anything else, qualified with merit, his mentors noting he had been born to be a journalist.

Eddie Boyle had found his calling, he had craved for excitement and found it in the world of journalism. Here, he flourished, walking the streets, day after day searching for that one special story, the one that would take him to the top.

Good looks, confident manner and outright charm parted closed lips like a chick feeding her young. No scandal happened that he wasn't aware of. No weather he wouldn't be out in, no avenue left untrampled.

Carrie backed her spouse to the full, pregnant with their first child, she suffered. Long hours she spent alone as she watched him win accolade after accolade, gaining local celebrity.

Tall at 6'3", dressed in his favoured brown corduroy trousers, blue woollen jumper and sneakers, Eddie had a smile for everyone he passed. They had a smile back. Eddie Boyle had a genuine interest in people. He cut through crap in an instance. His sparkling blue eyes all seeing his sharp brain, all knowing.

With so many female admirers, most wives would show jealousy, not Carrie. She was special. The only bed Eddie Boyle would climb into at night was hers. Not that it stopped him playing the field, pushing back his thick blonde hair when in the company of a pretty lady, winking as they blushed, loving every minute of their embarrassment.

Black camera hanging by his side, its many secrets hidden from sight. A5 Notepad in hand, small lead pencil tucked behind an ever-cocked ear, Eddie Boyle had the World in front of him. Say his name to anyone in Castleton and it would bring forth a gush of admiration. Talk of his kindness, his enthusiasm for his work surpassed only by talk of his love for Carrie, his wife of four years.

Locals would talk about his love of excellent food but smile about his ability to get the most out of people. His questioning technique, direct and probing. His knack of knowing an excellent story when he saw one of his compassion and discretion, all made him unique as a reporter.

Eddie Boyle published nothing for which he didn't have permission, or which would damage his sources. Such loyalty rewarded with a steady stream of solid information. If it happened in Castleton, he was on it. and was at the scene within minutes.

TORMENTED

Hot on the heels of awards came job offers from the Big City, a colonial reporter's dream. Happy with his lot but enticed by offers of big money, flattered Eddie. The lure of bright city lights seduced Carrie. An end to scrimping and saving appealed to her. A local reporter's pay was adequate but lacking when compared to the Big Nationals.

Wealthier for the years spent in the City, with an addition to the family, they returned to Castleton, wiser, happier and relieved. Back on familiar territory, the Boyle's settled once again into Castleton life.

Eddie, with renewed celebrity status, was now a genuine asset to any news office and was soon back, doing what he loved best, walking the streets, ears open, eyes peeled. Back digging out an excellent story, yet blind to the impending events that would turn his world into a living nightmare.

PATRICIA A SUTCLIFFE

Malcolm Ellis

Bleary eyed, Eddie picked up the phone. He had tried to ignore it, but its persistence had refused to let him. He no longer cared who was cheating on whom or which shop had been broken into. 'Just fucking let me rest in peace, will you?' he muttered, lifting it to his ear.

The urgency in the words of Bobby Brooks voice made the hair on Eddie's neck stand up on end. He let the phone drop, stood a minute to take stock. Had he heard right? He wasn't sure another body found her in Castleton. Cut up, a man, Malcolm Ellis, a loving family man with no axe to grind with anyone. No.... There had to be a mistake. 'Bobby wouldn't make a mistake!'

Eddie dug around for his notepad, pen and camera. He had no time to lose. He must get there before the nationals. See what was happening. Were there any witnesses to interview? Dotty, his wife. How was she? Questions were racing around his head. Dead, dead, no. Found in an alleyway. Eddie's thoughts were racing. He dashed from the building, his old instinct for a good story kicking in, driving him forward. This was a big one. He had to sober up.

Baker Street was crawling with police cars. Onlookers and other members of the press were gathering. Eddie headed straight for Bobby Brooks, who, looking flustered, his brow furrowed in consternation, was rubbing his temples. Together they looked at the scene in disbelief. Their eyes met, the old partnership back. Eddie didn't need to speak, he was aware of what Bobby Brooks was thinking,

They cordoned each end of the alleyway off, experts in white coats crawled about in the covered area like ants swarming over a kill. A white tent covered the exact place where the body lay, keeping it far away from prying eyes. The only story Eddie would get today he wouldn't find here.

Two murders in five months. This was beyond a coincidence. The first passed off as a gay killing, a tragic argument. The second killing, a married family man. This was more.

Roads were being cordoned off; Eddie forgot what was happening at the scene. He was already eyeing up the windows of the terraced houses that looked onto the back streets. He was in full reporter mode now, planning his theories, questions, answers.

Was the MO the same? There would be no useful press release until the autopsy was completed. It would be hours before forensics had finished scouring the scene. Wasted time to someone like Eddie. 'Anything to give me Bob. A name, a lead?' Bobby was saying nothing. It didn't bother Eddie. He would know when there was anything to release. Being here sufficed, his first report already at the Gazette.

On automatic pilot, Eddie mingled amongst the crowd, listening to the whispering emanating from the locals. As he focussed on the face of the throng, he noticed Susan Teal, a good reliable gossip.

He pushed through the wall of shaking heads and shocked faces to reach her. Beckoned her to the side. 'What are they saying, Sue?' his voice low and quiet. 'Talk to Netty Walsh if you can Eddie, I saw her getting out of a police car. I think she found him; it upset her.'

Filled with gratitude, Eddie headed to George Street. He rapped hard on the bronze knocker. The cracked red pane on the front door rattled. He had to get Netty talking. He needed a good punt. She would be in shock, told not to talk, or give a statement to the press. Her family would be there by now. Called by the police to stay with her. He weighed up his options, saw the curtain twitch. He knocked again.

Netty Walsh, one of life's characters, was a pleasant looking 50 some year old. A long-standing friend of

TORMENTED

Carrie's, a regular in the Moon, Eddie would play on her sympathies to get his foot in the door. It worked. Nettie beckoned Eddie towards a well-worn gold brocade chair. With a flip of her hand, she waved her daughter from the room. A fire crackled in the black grate. The room was warm, welcoming visitors in from the cold.

Netty looked to be in a state of shock, hands folded in her lap as she sat facing him. 'It was awful Eddie, just awful.' Her face heavily lined, eyes downcast and glazed. 'Awful, awful, I'll never forget him lying there, never.'

Eddie opened his notepad and begin scribbling, his questions posed gently, reassuringly. She trusted him when he made a promise. He would print nothing without Bob's validation.

Netty reached an outstretched hand towards Eddie. He clutched it in his. Mutual pity filled them both. Eddie needed a break. If Netty knew anything, she would share it with him. Carrie's story was well known by all in Castleton. She was more than aware of how Carrie had been found, despite the tragic circumstances. She had empathy with Eddie, she also needed to talk to someone. A good listening ear, trustworthy even for a reporter, Netty could now unload.

As she did so, his pencil worked, shorthand scribble daubed across the page. Occasionally he stopped to comfort her, patting her hand, squeezing.

The MO was the same, Eddie revealed nothing. Netty continued at a pace, venting her fear, her frustration and anger. 'Poor soul, poor soul, he wouldn't hurt a fly, he just wouldn't. I've known him for years, years.' Eddie found it hard to separate facts from Netty's personal thoughts and feelings was difficult. He ploughed on, coaxing out the information bit by bit.

'I left for work, 6am on the dot. To do my cleaning at the Moon.' Eddie nodded for her to continue.

'Left by the back gate, I always do, it's shorter. I thought it was a big bag somebody had dumped. Almost fell over him. God, I wish it had been a bag. Poor man, I still can't believe it, I just can't.' Irritated, Eddie nodded again.

'Thought it was a drunk then. I stepped in the blood, it was sticky, smelt queer. Lucky, I didn't fall. I screamed. I remember screaming. I'll never forget his eyes Eddie, full of terror, I've seen nothing like that, never.' Tears welled up in her eyes, Eddie contemplated stopping.

'Eddie, he was cut, his pants open. Why were his pants open? He must have taken a leak in the alley. It was horrible, I swear I'll never forget that, never forget Eddie. Why, who? Malcolm, Malcolm Ellis,'

Aware of her deepening distress, her sobs becoming louder by the minute, Eddie stopped the interview, leaving Netty in the comforting arms of her daughter.

TORMENTED

Chilly air rushed up to meet him as he stepped back into the street.

Some details were gruesome, making him grimace as he noted them down. He had fought to hold back his own tears, trying to keep himself pulled together. Images of Carrie hanging lifeless flooded his mind.

Netty would never forget her ordeal; he, better than most, knew that. She would remember this for the rest of her life, nothing would erase the visions that would haunt her.

He tried to shake his thoughts back to the job in hand, wiping his eyes, blinking. Malcolm Ellis; why? His thoughts moved to Tilly, Malcolm's wife. How would she be right now? Did she realise she could never fill the gap left behind?

Eddie Boyle was back in a black place, Carrie's body dangling in front of him. He needed a drink: his notes had to be collated. He made a mental note to speak to Tilly. Exhausted, he headed home. The Ellis family needed time to grieve. Eddie knew the drill; they would be protected. A police officer assigned to them before the nationals swooped on their prey like the vultures they were.

Buzzing around like a mob, no compassion, no morals. The juicier the story, the better. Eddie had been part of it and hated the savagery of it. Bobby's team wouldn't let that happen to one of their own, he knew that.

Scotch flowed like nectar, smooth and warm, quenching his thirst. It hit the spot. Eddie sat in the snug in the same seat Carrie always sat in, to be near to her, hidden from view from the principal bar area.

He stared at the photos on the wall depicting the pub's regular outing over the years. Listened to the chatter of the women, saw Carrie laughing, red lips pouting. Wavy red hair pinned back into a bun. Earrings dangling down, a birthday present from him.

The walk home, singing, befuddled, a little too much alcohol in the system. Eddie closed his eyes to linger on the memories, broken only by the thick Irish voice of Sean the landlord.

'The beggars were all over here, just missed em lad. Animals they are. Asked me so many fucking questions, I went dizzy. Anything to get the crack, they did. Cheeky bastards.'

Its peeved Sean, his voice heightening as he carried on his tirade against the nationals.

'I just ignored em, told em nothing. Who do they think they are? Even offered to pay me for the low down on Malc. What! The feller is a regular, one of us. Nice lass, his wife. I'm not filling their fucking papers for any price.'

They police hadn't released a name yet, and Eddie sensed they wouldn't. He had the advantage; he would use it.

Sean MacManus, landlord of the Moon, was a miserable man, small, slim, never a smile for anyone but loyal to his regulars. A lifeless man who had lost his heart for the job a long time ago. One too many drunks, fights and insults. The club behind the bar used too many times than he cared to remember. All had turned him into the dull, soulless man he was.

He broke off the conversation, Eddie answered the buzzing phone in his pocket. Malcolm Ellis confirmed Bobby Brooks. 'I'll be informing the nationals soon. They have called a news conference for 4pm.' Eddie had to move fast.

Two burly, old school policemen stood outside of Tilly Ellis's modest terraced house. Eddie only imagined the pain that lay beyond the guarded door. The church clock struck four, the news conference would take place, once done the buzzards would hover like vultures waiting for the kill. They would descend on George Street like bees to honey, straight to the door he was now looking at.

He needed the exclusive. By the time he clicked end, on his phone, he was disgusted in himself. He had used tactics learned in the City to get an interview with Tilly.

He knew the way the nationals operated, the enticements they offered. A picture he had clearly painted for the sobbing women. Explained to her, how they would insinuate on the reason the body was found in an alley in a state of undress.

How they would pull and twist the truth to sell their papers. How it was important that people read the truth, the loving family man Malcolm Ellis was. Desperate to safeguard the name of her husband, Tilly agreed to speak to him.

White nets, crisp and clean, were all there was to see of the front room. Beyond them, drawn green curtains. Eddie entered the passageway; The darkness of the grief mingled with the odour of bleach. Tilly Ellis was more than house-proud, brought about when Malcolm, a butcher, picked up a germ from a slaughtered beast. It had almost killed him. The Ellis's had been paranoid about cleanliness since.

The parquet floor beneath his feet creaked. He slipped off his shoes, calling out to Tilly. Hannah, Malcolm's first born, appeared from the living room, beckoning him to follow her.

TORMENTED

Several close relatives huddled around the small room, hugging each other. Tilly, eyes red and puffed, tears flowing, nodded to Eddie.

Eddie hesitated, sat himself by her side and sank into the deep-cushioned sofa. 'I don't know what to say, Tilly. I can only offer my deepest condolences.' Hannah slipped her hand around her mother's shoulder. They were together in their grief.

Cups and saucers were dotted about the room, some untouched, others half full. No one was interested in tea. 'I'm sorry Tilly, I'll come back another time'. Tilly, knees, red from kneeling as she scoured the front step each day, shook her head. She wanted to speak, to get the real story told. 'Talk about Malcolm, who he was. I want you to do that, I owe it to him.'

Eddie half smiled, took out his notepad and flicked over the page. Tilly spoke. He squeezed her hand. He saw how downtrodden she looked. Her head bowed; she was a total contrast to Malcolm. Small, slim, smartly dressed, down to the plaid slippers with little pom-poms and black Lyle stockings. Hair in a neat bun fastened with an ornate comb, greying at the roots, cupped her weathered face.

Unlike Malcolm, Tilly wasn't a drinker and rarely came to the Moon with him, content to let him have his own time. He would always be home at a decent hour. Always full of stories about the pubs, more colourful characters or how Sean MacManus had thrown somebody out. Tilly enjoyed the time to herself, encouraging his friendships. He would always be in bed by her side by 11.30.

Last night was different. She spoke about her anxiety come 11.30 and no sign of him. 'I phoned the police at 1am, I told them me concerns. They pacified me with a don't worry, he'll be back.' Reassured, she had retired for the night. They were right, he was probably settled in a lockdown game of cards. Forgot to ring her. That had to be it.

His key would turn in the lock at any moment, he would be full of apologies, full of remorse. She would scold him, chastise him. Re-assured Tilly had drifted into a restful sleep.

'Why?' her eyes implored Eddie to give her an answer. There was no answer forthcoming. Hannah took up the story. Tilly now sobbing, head held in her hands. She gushed with admiration for her father, how he would help anyone, give meat away. Give bargain cuts to the elderly at Christmas, break up trouble if he saw it. A regular family man who put his children and wife first. A fun-loving man of the community, playing Santa Claus every year at the local school. Malcolm Ellis was, to everyone, a God-fearing man of the Lord who would give his life for his family.

He may have tried to stop a fight, got in the way?' 'Maybe, I just don't know.' Remarked Eddie. The scenario of his death was pure conjecture but pure conjecture that the family at least could live with.

He would do everything in his power to show Malcolm Ellis for the loving family man he was. Pressing send, Eddie closed his eyes. He needed to sleep. He was sober!

Theories were rife. The nationals were having a field day. The Castleton Gazette, the only paper with any factual story, any real information about Malcolm Ellis. Some suggested that the first murder, a gay bashing gone wrong, was not linked to this case. The victim, single, effeminate, dressed in bright orange slacks, pale yellow jumper and trainers when found, fitted the profile of a gay man.

An unknown man, nobody locals cared about. Suggestions were made, reasons for him being in the Town, a pickup visiting, no one came forth with any proper explanations and anyone who knew anything, was saying nothing. The initial shock soon died down, long forgotten until now.

Malcolm Ellis was different, hugely different. Well respected, well known. The story that he had been breaking up a fight. A hero stabbed for helping another. Eddie suspected there was more to it. His senses were tingling the more he learned. He would find the truth. Get justice for Malcolm and Billy Ellis.

He would start at the Moon, see if he'd been drinking there, what time he arrived, left. Anything goes on in the bar, anyone sees anything. If anyone could understand it, it would be Eddie Boyle. He was buzzing with anticipation at solving this one. First call would be Bobby Brooks. He would say if anything unusual had been found on the body. Anything untoward that pointed to the killer?

TORMENTED

The Visit

Angel followed the story closely in the media, watching with interest the appeal for witnesses. The papers were rife with assumptions, theories, who, why, Castleton! All of them without facts, all of them wrong.

Only her father's article did she pay any proper attention to. She sneered at the description. A loving family man, portrayed as a hero, a saint. She laughed at the lies. Who were they kidding? Malcolm Ellis was anything but a loving family man, Malcolm Ellis was a dirty, low life, a decrepit bastard who needed only a skin full of ale to turn him in a lusting slob with rape on his mind.

Angel needed more information, a lot more information. Who was leading the investigation, what did the police think? Her father, Eddie Boyle, was a man who would best give her the answers. It was time for a visit.

Not knowing what she would find, Angel turned the key and entered her father's house, the home they had all shared. Expecting to find Eddie pissed and slumped on the floor, it surprised her to see him sitting in his chair typing.

The stench of alcohol still hung in the air, cigarette butts lie around the floor, the ashtray overflowing but no sign of the Jack Daniels. The brand of whisky her father favoured.

Startled by the figure of his daughter standing in the door frame, he spun round, knocking papers to the floor. He smiled, moved to embrace her. She stepped back avoiding the contact.

After they exchanged pleasantries, she remarked at how well he looked. His heart saddened; it wasn't true. Smiling at his daughter, he observed how much she looked like Carrie. He wanted to tell her how much he loved and longed to make it up to her. The coldness in her eyes told him she would never forgive him.

Eddie, desperate to enter a normal conversation, enquired about her latest book. She avoided answering; he would never be allowed into the innocence of the magical world she lost herself in when needing sanity. 'Ok'. The reply was bitter.

He changed tack, continued in his attempts to engage her. 'I'm pleased you're back in Castleton, I don't like it when you're touring. I'll visit if you like, proof your work, save you money.' She didn't need to reply, didn't need to involve herself in small talk. She was here for a reason, it had nothing to do with mending relationships.

'So, the killing?' Eddie's eyes flickered. 'Don't concern yourself with that, it's not pleasant.' Clever at feigning her fear, Angel gave an impression of being scared to be out on the streets alone, Eddie moved into protective father mode, assuring her she would be safe: Lying to her that the police thought it was linked to a vendetta against gays. 'The killer was after men, not women, you are safer than I am'. He wasn't convincing.

Angel had no intention of letting go, she pushed for more information. 'Why? The last victim was married.' Ever careful to relay only what had been published, she dug deeper. 'Bobby Brooks is leading the investigation, he confided in me that the body had been cut. The number 32 carved into his chest. Means nothing, no ideas why. They have someone working on it.'

'Surely there were some clues?' her voice low and innocent. Eddie looked hard at Angel, seeing in her place Carrie. Same colour hair, same blue eyes, same mannerisms even down to the graceful walk Carrie had. He wanted to be proud of her, tell her so, but she wouldn't allow him the contentment of acting the father role.

In the same way, she wouldn't share with him her real reasons for returning to Castleton or let him into the secret life she led. He would never understand.

Eddie longed to see his daughter more, but he had to go at her pace. Too pushy and it would be over. She seemed interested in the article he had written, for that he was pleased. If that's what it took to keep her, that's what he would talk about.

'Did you like my article? Poor Tilly Ellis was distraught, so sad. A similar MO to the first, same type of killing. Stabbed straight to the heart, he must be strong to do that in one move'.

'Any forensics?' Angel's questions were short but pointed. 'Nothing other than a single knife stab to the chest. The killer knows his business, knows how to inflict a fatal wound. Knows where to take his victims. They think he had been lying in wait, but why, that's the mystery. These men were nothing alike. No pattern at all.'

Angel was pleased. Her careful preparation had paid off. 'How anyone could kill another human being?' Her voice lacked conviction. He moved to her side, attempted to put his arm around her, she sidestepped. He missed holding her, he needed her, wanted her to need him.

Carrie's suicide had greatly affected Angel. He understood why she thought she had been betrayed, deserted by someone she trusted. Alone in a World she didn't want to be in. He shared her torment, loathed the way she looked at him. Her disgust. His shame at the state of his appearance.

Eddie Boyle needed to change; he would change. Claim his daughter back. Get back to the conversations they used to share. The way she used to kiss his forehead before bed each night. This was his chance, the case that brought him back, one to get his teeth into, take him to the top again? Gain her respect, give him back his own self-respect.

Angel's voice cut through his thoughts. 'Nothing at all to give them clues?' Eddie was about to tell his daughter more; he didn't want to. She didn't need the gruesome details. Still she persisted, 'Nothing, no fingerprints, no weapon. Something must have been found.' Angel was aware of the confusion on Eddie's face. He was struggling with what information to share and what he didn't want to. She turned towards the door. 'The angle of the blade meant the man was taller than the victim and strong judging from the depth of the wound.' Eddie shot the words at her, turning she softened. References to the killer being a man pleased her.

Eddie's next comments didn't. 'They found white particles on the wall, think it's from a jumper.' She blew him a fly away kiss, opened the door and prepared to leave. There were things to do. To take anything for granted, dangerous. She had exhausted the conversation.

'Don't go yet love, have a cuppa, a chat, it puzzles Bob, this one. I've not seen him so confused. The first one was gay, this one wasn't'. Angel had stopped listening. Her deep blue eyes settled on the bedroom door. A door she never wanted to enter again. Beyond that door lay her worst memories, memories she didn't want to revisit.

Beyond that door also lay the door to her own bedroom, unchanged since a child. The one painted pink: she had painted it herself, supervised by her mother. Stuck on the white doorplate with lilac flowers. It was still there. It looked out of place against the other doors. Now, it annoyed her. Another reminder of what was lost.

Next to Angel's room was their room. The room he had shared with her mother. The room was now locked, its contents hidden, not forgotten. Her father choosing to sleep in the lounge, a cheap, uncomfortable pull-down bed, his preference.

Angel understood why he had moved out of the large bedroom; why he hadn't moved into hers, she didn't understand.

Eddie did, the chance she might sleep over, if only for a night, was there. It was a dream that only he shared. Any hint of staying over angered her. Drew a reaction from her. Why would she want to stay, living as her father, immersed in that night? The thought triggered a coldness that built up inside of her, her instinct always to bolt.

She had all she would get from him today, nothing was stopping her going, nothing except the pity she experienced. This was new to her, an emotion to keep hidden. Unsettled, she accepted his offer of a drink.

Thick black coffee swam in the cup. She sipped a little, put it down. Thanking him, she looked at the papers strewn across the table, folded over at the articles he had written. A unique style to that of the nationals. To them selling papers came first, emotive headlines sold papers whether they were true. Eddie wrote factually, too close to his sources to betray them.

She focussed on the lined face of her once handsome father; the reality hit her. It hadn't been just her mother she had lost, but also her father. Now the home she loved, nothing but a dark place, a place devoid of light and laughter.

'I've let things go, Angel'. Eddie tried again to strike up a normal conversation with his daughter. 'I'm trying to get back on track, I'm trying for you Angel, I am. Give me a chance.' The words flowed over her; they didn't matter. Revenge, the only thing she focused on, the only thing that kept her going, the reality of her life.

Ashamed, he bowed his head. He wanted to change, recover his dignity. His position on the Gazette was the one thing he had left. A story like this, to bring him back from the abyss he had wallowed in. Who was he kidding, only the renewed love of Angel had the power to bring him back? A good father once, Carrie's death had consumed him, eaten away at him. Hiding emotion was now hard for him. He knew she blamed him for her mother's death. Why not, he blamed himself?

Angel was frustrated. She wanted more about the forensics, more about Bobby Brooks feelings, what had he shared with her father. More than he was saying for sure. 'How do you murder another a person?' Eddie, taken aback, turned. 'Why would you ask me that? I do not understand. I've never killed a person.' An icy stare accompanied his words. His thoughts were different. 'Anyone, if pushed far enough, if the motive was strong enough.' It was a question he had asked himself several times since Carries death.

Eddie Boyle had dark thoughts in his mind. Willingly, he would kill the perpetrators of Carrie's attack. Make them suffer as they had made him suffer. Take from them the most precious thing they owned. Without remorse or regret.

Angel's voice sliced through his thoughts like a knife. No answer was forthcoming. She saw his confusion, changed the subject. 'My recent book, you asked about it, it's almost ready for publication.' A tear sprang from his eye, his pride in his daughter too much to hide. He wiped it. She had seen it. Said nothing.

TORMENTED

Amazed at the way Angel handled the death, fears that it would destroy her as it had him, unfounded. She was strong, she had coped well. He had something to be grateful for.

A trembling hand told Eddie Boyle his craving had returned, the hidden bottle needed to resurface. Mindful of the rarity of the visit, he must wait. To cause alarm in any way unacceptable. '32 means what then?' The conversation moved back to what interested her. The profiler will tell us more.

They're setting up an incident room, Town square, I think.' The quizzical look she was getting from her father caused her to move away from him. Settling in Carrie's green chair by the fire grate, she hoped she hadn't pushed too far for information.

'How long before you kill yourself then?' She was pointing the rug burns where he'd dropped cigarettes whilst drunk. Nodding, he hung his head. An awkward silence ensued broken abruptly as he began a monologue, spewing out praises for the latest victim. Angel's iciness shocked him. She stared in silence. Her thoughts elsewhere. Eddie mistook her silence for attention.

'You don't understand, I have nowhere to turn, I don't want to live like this. Ashamed that you look at me the way you do. I love you; Really love Angel.' Pouring out his feelings was something new to him, but if his daughter understood a fraction of his words, he would make progress. He wasn't, Angel was in her own World.

A World of contradictions swinging between despair, hope, grief, longing. She wanted to yell at him, he had replaced the remnants of the perfume her mother wore with the odour of cheap whiskey and beer. She resented him for this. Longed to sense her mother's presence. Would it be there, behind that door? She was far from ready to find out.

Forgive me, Angel?' The words cracked through her thoughts, a whip flick bringing her back to painful reality. 'I don't blame you'. She lied. She noticed how he clasped his hands to hide the shaking. It wasn't working. Unable to halt his tear ducks, they overflowed, tears collected in the corners of his swollen eyes.

His obvious stress stirred an emotion inside of her, an emotion she preferred not to have. She wanted to retreat. Leave him to his own sorrow as he had left her to hers.

To show him compassion, a step too far. Gaining strength together too much for her to bear. She left him standing in the centre of the gloomy room as she made her departure.

Slumped in Carrie's chair, a heavy ache entombing his heart, Eddie reflected on the conversation. It took one hour with his daughter, 60 minutes, to make him so low he just wanted to join Carrie. He found it hard to come to terms with the iciness in his daughter's eyes, his feelings of total abandonment. He focussed his mind back to the murders. His opportunity to prove himself.

It hit him like a brick, his heart lifted. Why would she visit? How stupid. She wanted to build back what they had lost so suddenly. Take an interest in his work? It was her way of holding out an olive branch. Conviction filling his head, Eddie Boyle drifted asleep. The whiskey bottle remained hidden.

PATRICIA A SUTCLIFFE

Carrie Boyle

Carrie Boyle, a unique woman, known by all, loved by most, misunderstood by some. Some refused to see beyond the smart City clothes. Saw them as too fancy for Castleton. They were the ignorant, the envious who failed to see the outgoing, fun loving mother. A mother full of adoration for her daughter. Devoted to her husband, her beauty as deep on the inside as it was as obvious on the outside.

Daytime saw Carrie busying herself around her top-floor apartment. A stark contrast to the two up, two down she and Eddie had begun their married lives in. Polishing, dusting, arranging, cooking. A meal ready on the table to greet Angel and Eddie. A smile and a word of encouragement on her lips.

Carrie stopped only to check she looked her best, her lipstick fresh, hair in place, she loved her routine. Mealtimes were exacted with precision, white cloth, smoothed across the polished table. Cutlery placed just so, everything as it should be, like Carrie, everything had to be perfect down to the fan folded napkins.

TORMENTED

Carrie's life had been as neat as her table. A wardrobe for day clothing, a wardrobe for evening clothing. She loved the nights out with Eddie, always ending up in the Moon. The transformation from smart, urban housewife to glamorous companion was something she achieved with ease. She looked young for her years, Carrie had lost none of her allure, until that fateful night, that is.

She prided herself upon her appearance, the same red hair her daughter had inherited. Tied in a neat bun during daytime, long and loose by the evening. Carrie Boyle had everything to live for, never failing to get a second glance wherever she went. Such attention didn't go unnoticed to Eddie, ever proud, seeing the looks his wife got as a compliment to his excellent choice of partner.

Together they made a handsome couple, a couple worthy of envy from the narrowminded, bilious women of Castleton who had let themselves go. The same women whose husbands eyed up females like Carrie Boyle and envied men like Eddie. Angel was extremely fortunate, boasting the best features of both parents.

Occasionally, Eddie and Carrie would venture into Town, but the Moon remained their favourite haunt, Tuesday's and Thursday's darts and domino nights. August 21st had been one such night. A balmy summer evening, stars hung like crystals in the sky's stillness. Carrie got ready for a night in the snug. Eddie prepared for his match.

PATRICIA A SUTCLIFFE

The bar was full, a lot of strangers gathered for the singles championship. Missing out the year before in a three-dart finish, Eddie was hoping to carry the cup away this time. The atmosphere tense but friendly. Beer flowing.

Carrie took up her usual seat in the snug, the one by the door. This was the lady's domain. Men didn't venture into the snug, few women ventured into the bar on a match night. Mixed events were reserved for the concert room where couples mingled and danced to the entertainment every third Saturday in the month. Popular with visitors and regulars alike, the concert room saw foul mouthed men transformed into loving husbands and delighted women showing off their finery.

Like most Victorian Public houses, the snug was a small room, warm and cosy, an odour of perfume, a sharp contrast to the rowdy, sweaty odorous bar with its colourful language. Here the women laughed, told private stories, belittled their men's prowess in the bedroom. Complained about their lack of energy, lack of money and lack of anything else they recalled.

A normally, cheerful Carrie didn't feel well, just a minor headache, nothing a good night's sleep wouldn't cure. He wanted her to share his glory, she knew that. His determination to win the cup strong, Eddie persuaded her to get ready. Much against her better nature, Carrie gave in, donned her glad rags and smiled at her grateful spouse.

TORMENTED

'You look great, fantastic.' Dressing in her tight red dress, low at the neckline, just short of knee-length, made her feel good. She liked to look the part. Tonight, she would have changed for a long warm nightgown and a comfortable pillow. She finished applying the deep red lipstick she always wore, she was ready. 'Come on love, you'll enjoy it once we're there. Free sarnies, drinks flowing and me winning the cup.'

Ever proud of his achievements, knowing how much a victory would mean to him, wanting to encourage him? She smiled. She had to support her man.

By 8.30pm the bar was buzzing, matches were underway to the cheers of the regulars drowning out the barracking emanating from the losing away team. Copious drinking, noise decibels rising, Carrie's head was now pounding. By 10 o'clock a migraine, something she had suffered with since giving birth to her daughter Angel, was in full swing. Carrie felt sick, even the smallest whisper now sounded like a hammer drumming on her skull.

Carrie needed fresh air, whispering to her closest friend. 'Tell Eddie I have a migraine; I'll see him at home.' She picked up her white coat, stood and quietly slipping out. Eddie too engrossed in his game to notice.

The cool air on her face was welcome, an instant relief. Should she call a taxi, she decided against it. The brief walk would do her good. The short jacket pulled round her, she stumbled on the cobbles, the only area she didn't like crossing in heels. A couple stood across the road, kissing by an alleyway lamp. Half-heartedly, she smiled, recalling the days when she and Eddie had done the same.

Except for a group of men talking loudly on the opposite side of the road, Baker Street was empty. Aware of the jeering and smut coming from their mouths as she passed, she ignored them. She avoided looking across at the men, quickened her pace and continued her journey.

Her heart quickened. They had crossed the road behind her, were now following her, chanting at her. The taunts echoed, breaking the silence. Panic setting in, she looked for lights in windows as she passed the terraced houses. She would knock on the door, pretend to be going there. Lewd songs were now being sung in unison. The Moon wasn't that far away. Should she go back? It meant her walking through the group.

Fear welled up in her, she sensed danger. They had gone quiet, whispered to each other. She shook. Looked back, the couple were gone; it was now deserted. Her heart sank. They rounded on her, surrounded her, pushing and pulling her towards an alleyway, her attempts to scream silenced by a thick hand holding her mouth tightly. Terror mounted in her, another arm grabbed hers, swinging her around violently.

TORMENTED

Half dragged, half carried, they pulled her past the back gates, past lit back rooms, deeper and deeper into the darkness of the alley.

Hands grabbed at her breasts, pulled at her clothing, fingers tearing, ripping at her undergarments, all the while the thick hand pressed harder across her mouth. Her breathing now becoming difficult, she got dizzy. A hand twisted her ponytail hard, forcing her to the ground. For a moment, the grip loosened on her mouth. She let out a muffled scream.

A fist hit her hard in the face. Blood gushed from her mouth and nose. 'Shut it slag'. A face leaned close to hers, the alcohol infused breath overpowering her. She vomited, choking, another fist jammed hard into her stomach. She doubled over, the vomit splattering. 'Dirty git, look at my fucking shoes.' She tried to look up, say sorry. Another fist hit her hard in the face. Her teeth smashed; her bones cracked.

Now on her knees, held down by several of the men, pain ran through her body as one by one they took a turn to rape and abuse her, pushing her into different positions. Harder and harder, pushing themselves into her body, forcing themselves on her, encouraged by the laughter of their accomplices. Humanity long forgotten.

Her entire body shaking, she tried to look at the faces, remember them. Thud, another fist landed with force, Carrie slumped, blacking out.

'Carrie, Carrie.' A soft voice sounded in the blackness of her thoughts. She fought to open her blackened, swollen eyes; the bright light hurt her. Pain filled her body; Her mouth fused with blood. It stopped her screaming, crying out. Defeated, she closed half-opened eyes. Images swamped her terrified mind. She let out a small gurgle. A hand touched her shoulder.

Carrie Boyle was broken, dead inside. Crushed and beaten, left for dead in a dirty back alley. Her life as a carefree, confident woman erased with every punch strike. Life for her, changed forever, her only constant companion now, fear. She was a blank. Only a pummelled, battered shell remained. Carrie Boyle was beyond recognition.

By her bedside, touching her limp hand, Eddie Boyle was sobbing, head hung down. Total shock filling his body, a silver trophy laying on the white tiled floor. 'Let me die'. Carrie Boyle whispered.

A police officer, disbelief etched on his face, stood guard in the corridor, opening the door to allow Bobby Brooks into the room. Carrie lay unrecognisable.

He placed a supportive hand on his friend's shoulder, he stood silently. The only reporter he had ever admired was now looking up, eyes swollen and red. He shook his head. 'We need to talk; I have to ask some Questions.' Kissing Carrie's battered face, Bobby held his arm and led him to a small room. 'I'll find the bastards; I promise I'll find them'.

'Why? She didn't want to go, I fucking pushed her to. See me get a cheap fucking cup. For what? She had a headache, a fucking headache but me, no, it had to be about me, had to have her there when I won. Poor cow, what do I say to her, what do I do? I didn't realise she'd left some fucking husband. A darts match meant more to me. I'll never forgive myself, never. What am I going to do, Bob?'

'We will find who did this pal, I promise you both that'. Nothing he said would ease the pain Eddie was going through. Bobby was aware of that. He still needed answers, had to push.

'What time did she leave the pub?'

'She's smashed up bad Bob. They broke her jaw, her eye socket, her teeth, the bastards. She didn't have a chance, no fucking chance. Why the fuck didn't she wait for me. Another hour, just another hour. How do I tell Angel? Angel can't see her like this, she can't'.

Eddie's voice was becoming erratic, loud, panicked. Then, eyes staring into space, he appeared to become calm.

'I Heard the sirens Bob, they said a fight had gotten out of hand, some fucking idiots, too much to drink. I'm a reporter, I had to go look. Never forget what greeted me. Her coat was on the floor, soaked with blood. They had her in the ambulance. They were working on her, she was groaning, fucking groaning, I didn't understand. I'll never forget that noise. That sound.'

'wanted to run, it was my Carrie, I didn't want it to be, but it was her. They let me travel with her, but they said not to touch her. I thought I'd lost her. I didn't recognise her as my beautiful wife Bob, didn't recognise her. Look at her. What they did, why? Will she die, Bob?'

Eddie's voice was pleading. His friend shook his head showing a negative. The interview, pointless.

'We'll do this later. when you are more up to it. We'll do everything we can, everything to find the bastards who did this, everything. Angel, has she been told?'.

Eddie shook his head. We have to keep her from this.'

Normally, Bobby would seek Eddie out for information, the lowdown on the streets. He would get more out of any witness than the police. This time it would be different. He would limit the usual sharing of information to known facts. No assumptions made. No stone unturned.

Laden with guilt. His wife was lying motionless. The crisp white sheets a start contrast to the deep red swelling of what was once, her face. Her eyes barely open, the pain so great that his helplessness angered him, tore him inside. Her words stinging him to the core. 'I'll go for you Eddie; but you owe me one'.

Her words resounded in his head. He'd been angry when he realised, she had left early, left before seeing him achieve victory. Annoyed, thought her selfish, wanted to tell her so. Would tell her so. He slumped to the floor, hands on his head, overcome with tiredness and grief. He sobbed, howling like a beaten dog. Broken and beyond help.

A fractured eye socket, three cracked ribs, two broken teeth, a broken jaw line, a broken nose, internal and external bruising of both vagina and anus., Bobby Brooks found it hard to comprehend the injuries and slammed down the medical report. Carrie Boyle was a selfless soul. This shouldn't happen to someone like her, it shouldn't happen to anyone, but someone like her. The attack, vicious, vile, prolonged. Carried out by more than one culprit.

He needed answers, need answers fast, but experience told him it would not happen. Carrie was too fragile to interview. Her body needed to mend, but her mind was a different being. It may never mend.

Bobby had seen assault victims carry the mental scars far longer than the physical ones. This, one of the worst attacks he'd seen, would be life changing. She may never recover.

Determined to find the culprits, put them away for a long time, he had ordered every spare copper out, searching for answers, clues that would move the case forward.

No amount of tender probing, smiling, gentle arm stroking coaxed Carrie to re-live the attack. Her only utterances, there were at least three of them, she had passed them; they had followed her. Her words, matter of fact, cold, repetitive. Details of the attack itself remained locked in the deep caverns of her psyche. Descriptions of the men were vague. Nothing seen, came from behind, too dark. Memory lapses didn't help. Her thoughts unclear, the night a blur after the first punch.

The police knocked on doors, examined the scene with a fine-tooth comb, it did nothing to ease the frustration mounting in Castleton police station. They had little evidence. The only real witness, the victim herself, repeating only the original utterances made to Bobby Brooks at each interview attempt. Hours turned into days, days into weeks, weeks into months, still no breakthrough.

Carrie's return home, low key, unreported, guarded. Gone the strong, confident woman who had walked out that fateful night, returning, a weak, scared shell. Life would never be the same, Carrie's eyes were as empty as she was inside, her soul ripped out. Eddie desolate, his wife unrecognisable.

TORMENTED

Beyond Hope

Angel woken by a knocking that told her instinctively, it needed to be answered. Something was wrong. It was a formal official knock. She pulled a white silk robe around her slim body, fastened the belt. Checked the chain was on, opened the door and faced the grim faces of two police constables. What she heard next changed her life forever.

Perched on the edge of an expensive leather couch, a policeman holding her hand, Angel listened as the words spilled out. Only three heard. 'Mother found dead'. 'Mother found dead'. Words that resounded in her mind, touching her very being. 'Mother found dead'. A sentence that embedded itself deep with her. 'Mother found dead' words that echoed around the room like a record player, a needle stuck in the same groove. Numb in shock, nothing else registered.

'Father, what about father?'. She needed to be with him, support him, be there now. A deep anxiety overwhelmed her. She cried loudly, a long low moaning cry. Nothing seemed real. Her world gone. Her fundamental reason for existing, gone. Taken from her and she didn't understand why.

Despair blocked questions she would have asked, demanded to have answers to. Answers that would have made her blood run cold, draining any sense of emotion from her. It was as well she didn't.

She muttered a thank you to the officers, alighting their patrol car in front of her parents' home. The curtains were closed. Another police officer stood by the door. The two officers escorted her, stopping to whisper to their colleague. Her hand shaking, she reached for the knob. The hallway was in darkness, the door to the apartment ajar. She heard muffled voices. A figure in a white overall appeared before her, glanced at her and passed her by.

Her stomach in a tight knot, she felt sick and unsteady. An eeriness hung in the air, bringing a chill to the warm, welcoming home she loved visiting. The lounge was now silent, no sign of her father, but sobbing coming from a bedroom steered Angel towards the door. Something she didn't comprehend stopped her turning the knob, instead she listened. A gut-wrenching cry emanating from beyond the door.

'Mother found dead'. The words rung in her ears, bringing her back to reality. She pushed open the door; On the marital bed lay her father, tucked into a foetal position, her face hidden beneath his arms. Clutched in his hand Carrie's woollen shawl, the one she always pulled across her shoulders.

Angel wanted to rush to him, comfort him, Instead, she stood glued to the spot, her mother's scent lingering in the room. 'Father'. She spoke softly, approaching the form on the bed. Terror hiding the growing apprehension churning in the pit of her stomach. He didn't move, just laid there, his sobbing growing louder at the sound of his daughter's voice.

Her mind confused, she touched his shoulder, slumped down beside him and curled up. So many questions raced through her mind, she wanted answers, the questions stuck in her throat. One part of her aching for knowledge, another wanting nothing, wanting the last hour to be a nightmare she would soon awaken from. Back to where she was before a loud, intrusive banging had sent her to open her apartment door.

Away from home most of the year, doing book tours, readings and signings had protected Angel from the changes that had taken place in her mother over the past two months. She had known nothing of her mental or physical decline. Had she, her visits would have been more frequent.

Angel Boyle lived under the illusion that all was well, any idea that her mother would commit suicide as distant as her being anything but a children's writer. To her Carrie was a fun, loving, outgoing wife and mother, adoring her family and living for today.

Home had always been her sanctuary. Her place of safety when she had the need. An independent woman, it didn't arise often, the knowing was all that was necessary and gave her the confidence to move forward in life.

Her voice shaking with emotion, she reached to touch the shawl before recoiling back in horror. A white outline of a body chalked on the wooden floor a short distance from the doorframe. She squeezed her father's hand, struggling to understand why she had missed it when entering the room.

'Is, is that where…….', Her voice trailed off, Eddie already nodding.

Why? I don't understand, it makes little sense'. Eddie turned to face his daughter. Grief etched on his face, he looked old, different to when she had last seen him. Scared at her reaction, he told his daughter of the attack Carrie had endured. The injuries, how she had changed. The blame he endured, of the anger that filled him every day the perpetrators remained free.

Shocked, the thought of her mother, someone she loved, suffering at the hands of a bunch of filthy drunks, hurt her to the core.

TORMENTED

Her mother being raped, beaten, in pain, filled her mind.

She visualised them attacking her, anger welling up, knowing They were out there. Their lives being lived whilst her mother had lost hers. Were they attacking other women, getting away with it? Why? Why had they been allowed to walk free? It grated on her, incensed her! They wouldn't, she would make sure of that.

Shock turned to anger. Why hadn't she been told? She would have done something. Why wasn't she given the chance? Why did her father think he had a right to keep it from her?

Eddie, fighting to find his voice, explained how the police had done all possible but with no witnesses, no real evidence at the scene, Carrie unable to recall anything about the attack, it had been impossible to detain anyone.

'Why didn't you tell me the truth?'

The sadness in her father's eyes told her not to push for an answer, there would be time later.

Carrie had tried hard to come to terms with her horrific ordeal, to share

With her daughter, bring her family close to her side. Guilt, remorse, disgust with herself, all held her back. She remained. Trapped in her own closed world, refusing to bring the night back to her consciousness. The place she lived in, dark, stifling. Her fear at leaving the house, overwhelming and numbing.

Carrie needed to be safe. She did not understand who her assailants were. Thought they had followed her out of the Moon, targeted her. It frightened her more. The thought horrified her. Most of the men in there were friends, she laughed with them, trusted them, shopped with their wives, families. The thoughts tormented her, ate her up.

Every man walking past her on the street became a suspect, was one of them. Eddie tried everything. Nothing worked to allay Carrie's fears. Hour after hour she questioned herself, often until her head ached. Still no answers.

Why's filled her thoughts. Why had she set off alone? The match would have finished shortly. Why dress that way? Had she encouraged them? Were they laughing at her in the pub? Had they singled her out? Were known to everyone. Were they coming after her? What if they thought she had seen them, waiting for a chance to get to her? What would they do to silence her? Carrie lived in torment. The questions raced around her head, never pausing for breath.

TORMENTED

'I watched her, saw her slip more and more into depression. She didn't want to do anything, stopped wearing her lovely clothes. Stopped cleaning, stopped eating. I saw her losing weight, it was like she wasn't there. She just didn't hear me anymore. I tried Angel, I tried.'

Eddie exhaled. 'She neglected herself, started staying in bed, sometimes not getting up at all. Long into the night, I heard her crying. I wanted to hug her, put my arms around her, comfort her, but she didn't want me to touch her.

Angel saw the pain in her father's eyes, wanted to hold him, she resisted.

'I ached to love her more, make her well. It was useless, just useless. She wouldn't let me help. Beg as I did. I tried to tell her it would be okay, she pushed me away. Your mum lived in constant fear.'

For the first time Eddie Boyle was lost. Didn't know what to say. The woman he loved, disappearing deeper and deeper into herself each day.

On the odd occasions he had gone to the Moon, Carrie safely tucked up in bed, he found himself looking at the faces of men, studying them. Their crude jokes, raucous laughter, comments about women, now seemed sneering and dirty.

Interviewed by the police, some more than once, some angry at assumptions being made. Others, full of sympathy for Eddie and Carrie but not knowing what to say, avoiding discussion with him. Eddie stood alone, isolated, pushing him to leave early, go home to Carrie face more silence.

The alleyway where Carrie was found was on his route home. His heart almost broke every time he passed. He would look hard, see who was there. If anyone was lurking in the shadows. Anger boiling inside him, wanting to scream. In the prior days, days he had walked up and down looking for clues, finding nothing. He had been left dejected.

'I wasn't there for her, wasn't there. A fucking trophy meant more. I should have been there to help her; Should have heard her screams. I didn't, I let her down, Angel, I let her down and I'll never forgive myself. Now she's gone.' His voice apologetic, his head in his hands.

He needed his daughter's understanding, her forgiveness. He wouldn't get it. Anger filled her eyes. She flinched as Eddie tried to reach for her, making him recoil. Eddie stood, shaking, unsteady. He saw in Angel the same rejection he had faced from Carrie.

Angry at the suffering her mother had gone through, the lack of trust at not being told, at being left in the dark. She would have cut her book tour short, returned in an instance. Her stare became icy, glaring, unfocused. She hated the vividness of her own imagination, her ability to visualise her mother. She saw her struggling in terror, bleeding at the hands of a group of filth. One dirty, inky night had changed their lives forever.

Deep in the Ground

The cold midday mist hung over the graveyard as the sombre procession let its way up the hill to the oak tree beneath which Carrie would rest. A polished coffin carried by six pole bearers, adorned with a large silver cross, matching the casket handles. CARRIE BOYLE – 1st April 1958 – 7th October 2007 read the plaque in simple lettering, a vast contrast to its occupant in her heyday.

Heavy police presence matched only by the huge number of towns people, gathered to show their respect to the family. Several of the police officers on duty, alert to anyone acting suspiciously. Every mourner scanned, looking for suspects. Expertly eyeing up faces, memorising them.

A scene full of despair, Eddie shuffled behind the coffin, face drawn, eyes swollen, huddled against the cold. His long black overcoat, its collar pulled around the neck, covered his new black suit. Head bowed; his pain clear for all to take pity in.

Alongside, walked Angel, eyes darting from face to face, taking in the gathered crowd. Were the attackers there, watching, guilty, trying to keep suspicion away from them? It disturbed her. She wanted to scream for the bastards to show themselves, come forward. She wanted her mother to rise from the grave, point them out, haunt them forever.

In contrast to Eddie, Angel showed little obvious emotion. The stony stare she could give in an instance, refusing to reveal the turmoil inside. She reflected on the number of mourners that had filed into the small church, many of them regulars in the Moon. Heard the whispers, concerned comments, finger pointing, weak voices, some tearful and shaky.

Angel half smiled, recalling the vases full of Lilies, their scent drifting across the pews. Carrie would have approved, To Angel they were the flowers of death.

Intently listening, Angel grimaced at the vicar's meaningless words. What did he know of her mother? Nothing, zero. He rambled on, spoke about her in glowing terms, emphasising that this was a celebration of her life. She cringed as he gushed about God's forgiveness until his eyes met hers, his voice lowering to almost a whisper.

Her emotion locked inside, she listened in silence as her father make an impassioned speech. Watching him, sharing his pain, seeing his tears flowing down his shallow cheeks. Standing, leading him from the pulpit, gripping his arm, steadying him.

Angel had a deep need for answers to questions that burned into her senses, caused her stomach to twist into knots. Questions, never far from her thoughts, occupying her waking moments. Her sleeping hours brought no solace either, filled with visions of her mother's bloodied body, turning to see a contorted face, a body hanging from a rope.

Strength and need were all that were keeping Angel from her despair. A need for justice pushing her on. A mission so strong that only her own demise could end it.

Angel stared at the ground. She watched her mother's coffin disappearing into the blackness. Her eyes focussed on a worm wriggling its way out of the soil, causing bits of earth to drop onto the box. Its precious cargo lifeless, unaware.

How many of the morose faces, eyes ogling Eddie in pity. Hands resting on shoulders, comforting each other, were thanking God it wasn't them?

Within hours most of them would be drunk, telling stories, remembering the quality times. Alcohol flooding their blood streams, losing their defences. Compassion flowing, telling Eddie how they would be there for him. How they understood his pain and would do their best for him. He only had to ask. Such bullshit, hypocrisy. Angel always hated the way funerals unfolded. One-minute tears, kind words of sympathy, bouquets with gushing tributes followed by free food, flowing beer and a good time relaying story after story about the dear departed.

It was natural to Eddie to hold the wake in the Moon. To Angel it was grotesque. It seemed darker than she remembered. A fire crackled in the grate; the odour of ale hung in her nostrils. Would they dare be here, were they living in fear, waiting for the knock on the door?

The dart board, thousands of tiny holes piercing its well-played surface, hung 5 ft 8 inches from the floor. Her eyes shifted from the board to the snug where Carrie would have been sitting. She saw her father engrossed in his match, her mother slipping out of the heavy door unnoticed by him. Watched by her assailants, lust in their veins, ready to instil fear and terror into her heart.

She reeled as she listened to the condolences tumbling from stuffed mouths, the grease of pork pies washing down their throats. She took in the black-clad figures swooping down on the buffet, overfilled paper plates bending with weight. Beer spilling balanced in grabbing hands. She hoped they would choke.

The bar resembled a gathering of crows. Arms flapping, reaching for glasses, beaks opening, laughing, swilling alcohol down. How she hated them. How many would walk home, eyeing up attractive women? Where would their thoughts be now, with Eddie and his grief or in their pants, their hopes high for what the night would bring?

Eddie, drowning in a sea of emptiness, accepted pint after pint, his sorrows deepening with every mouthful. Angel sipped on a glass of fresh orange. Her mind deadened to the growing noise emanating from intoxicated figures. Their swaying bodies propped up by the bar rail.

Angel felt sickened as stories of Carrie and Eddie turned to smut filled jokes to lighten the mood. The tellers, getting their attempt to cheer Eddie up, so dramatically wrong.

Compelled to stay by her father's side, Angel wanted nothing more than to escape, but spotting Bobby Brooks across the room, she saw an opportunity. She approached. Reaching out to hug her, he beckoned her to sit. 'I need answers, Inspector Brooks'.

Her voice solemn. 'I need information. What have you found out about the men who attacked my mother, raped and beat her so she took her life?' Her eyes intense, Bobby nodded acknowledgment. 'I need answers.' Urgency hung on her words. 'Come down to the station tomorrow, Angel, we'll talk then'. Grateful, her hand touched his.

'Time dad lets go home now'. Eddie, unsteady on the cobbles, stumbled. Angel, strong and agile, caught him, prevented him from falling. Baker Street was quiet, a light drizzle in the air. They headed towards the Town Square, a short distance to the apartment block Eddie lived in.

Angel noticed a heaviness in Eddie's gait, how he shuffled, trying to keep pace with her long stride. Without speaking, she slowed as they reached level with the alleyway. Both looked in its direction but didn't stop.

Flashes of her mother swam in her mind. Taking this same path with her, kissing her cheek goodnight. Wonderful memories, gone too into darkness. Images of Carrie being dragged, half carried, hands grabbing at her. Did her father have the same visions? The same pain? Knowing the men who did this were free? Angel, the tight knots in her stomach aching, wanted to challenge him but saw the sorrow he carried, the guilt, the regret.

Passing through the park, having left her father sleeping, still dressed, a blanket thrown across him. Angel heard a voice calling to her.
'Angel isn't it, haven't seen you in years, you've changed.' Alarmed, she caught sight of a figure, sat on

the bench reserved for dealers. It was still early, too early for the druggies who frequented the park.

He appeared to be someone in need. 'You're a beauty, have to say'. Unimpressed by the falseness of his compliments, Angel said nothing. Normally, she would have walked straight on. Now she looked at him. A writer with a keen eye for detail, she weighed him up. Mid 30s, tall, dark brown eyes, wide mouth and a grin that said trouble.

A regular in the Moon maybe, she wasn't sure, so threw him a test. Watching his reaction, she told him that she had been to her mother's funeral. 'Carrie Boyle, do you know her?' He shuffled, murmuring a quick sorry. Stood and headed toward the Town, The look on his face one of shock. Angel noticed it, it unnerved her.

The pinched her face hard as she hurried from the park. Once across the road, she glanced around then entered the safety of her apartment. The blind flicked back she peered across at the park. An eerie quiet had descended,

She closed her eyes; a wave of unwelcomed imagery flooded her brain. She stood in the church yard. The blackness of her mother's grave looming up at her, the casket being lowered. Faces, faces swimming around her, nodding, touching hers, smothering her. Her mother's body, cold and alone. Stood motionless, her senses dead, emotions frozen, she took in the scene. Absolute emptiness filled her.

Angel opened her eyes. The emotion that had eluded her, would be released. Unseen, unheard. No one would see her weakness.

Angel had bought her apartment four years previously. Given thanks for the success of her first book. A year of constant searching, viewing apartment after apartment to find her ideal match. The place that would become hers, her cocoon. The heavy entrance door, her block to the outside World.

Once inside, she'd could create the characters she brought to life in her books. Here, at one with herself. Safe.

Encouraged by her father, the last few years had been spent as a travelling author. The delight on the faces of the little ones as she told her stories in packed school halls always treasured.

She welcomed the comments she received at her book launches, remained fascinated by the number of autographs signed. Excellent years, tiring, successful years, years she would kill to have back.

Now, success had little meaning for her. Justice was all that consumed her. It was her obsession. It ate at her flesh, picked at her sanity. Angel would now remain in

Castleton until justice was done, nothing but her own death would deter her from achieving her goal.

The park lay in darkness, figures moved about, alcoholics and druggies crept from out of the shadows. Their business there as dark as those who frequented it at night. A stark contrast to the daytime when the park teamed with school groups on nature runs. Its benches occupied by the elderly out for a stroll, but whose legs needed frequent rest. Their eyes filled with the pleasure, seeing youngsters play, their hearts envying their youth and vitality.

At night, the park took on a different appearance, a strange foreboding cast its net far and wide. Sounds of birds singing and children's laughter exchanged for moans and groans of ecstasy as illicit needles pierced punctured, bruised arms.

Angel spent many hours listening to the park at night, a place she once feared after dark. The events that led to her mother's death had changed all of that. Now she feared little, so narrow, the line between life and death. A harsh lesson learned forcefully.

Tonight, she longed for a walk through the park just one more time with Carrie. To enjoy again the private time they shared, walking, talking, putting the World to rights. The World would never be right again. Her mother now lay in a cold grave covered in soil, laden down the strong odour of rotting flowers.

TORMENTED

Angel never understood why mourners brought flowers to funerals. Perplexed by why they found it necessary to kill one species to show respect for the dead of another.

Overcome with the day's events, the weight of tiredness filling her body, Angel walked to her bedroom, her thoughts idling on tomorrow's meeting with Bobby Brooks.

A stony silence hung in the room as Angel listened to the details of her mother's attack. Forensics found evidence of semen but failed to find a match to any of the samples taken from the voluntary specimens of the Moon's clientele. 'We suspect a group visiting from out of Town rather than locals and we don't have enough evidence to bring anybody in and demand a sample.' Angel remained unconvinced but said nothing.

The conversation moved to her mother's suicide. Aware that the Inspector arrived early on the scene, Angel pushed for detail. 'How did you find my mother's body'? 'We need not go over it, all that matters are that I won't rest until we find who caused this'. Angel retorted, fast and smarting. 'I'm not a child, don't treat me like one. I want to understand; I have a right, she may be a case to you, to me she is, WAS my mother. '

An icy look told Bobby Brooks that the young woman before him meant business. 'She, your mother, hung a rope on a hook above the door, climbed on a chair and, we can only think, kicked it from under her. It would have been over quickly'.

'How the fuck can you assume that'. The words sprang out before Angel had time to stop them. The thought of her mother, so desperate, knocked a hook into the doorframe, knotted a rope, stood on a chair and kicked it from under her, sickened Angel to the core. She hated the power of her own imagination generating a now vivid image of Carrie dangling from a rope, gasping for air, turning blue in the face. A grotesque thought.

As if reading her thoughts, Bobby explained her mother's stomach content showed she'd consumed tablets before...... his words drifted away as he tried to spare Angel from unnecessary details. His attempts failed. Such avoidances served only to make her angrier and more determined that justice would be served.

Had she known; she would have helped her mother more. Talked her through the terrible times, reasoned with the state of her mind. Instead, she was too hung up in her career. She would have sympathised with her, made her realise it hadn't been her fault. Taken her away, eased her fears.

Why her father kept the details of the attack from her, she still didn't understand. Why wait to tell her now that her own mother's mind had disintegrating into despair? She failed to comprehend why her mother decided not to tell her anything? Perhaps she misunderstood their closeness. That pained her.

Angel shrugged Bobby Brooks hand from her, got up, left the room. That none of her parents confided in her stinging her senses beyond belief. She reasoned her mother wouldn't have been in a right state of mind, would have tried to protect her. No excuses existed for her father. She wouldn't forgive him, but she would use him, for however long, to exact revenge for her mother.

PATRICIA A SUTCLIFFE

Reality Hurts

Three years to the day of Carrie Boyle's death, the first body emerged. Bloodied and crumpled, it lay in a rain-soaked alleyway opposite the Half Moon Public House. The victim's bright orange trousers down to his knees, his pale-yellow jumper pulled up over his face. In the centre of his bare chest a zig zag of deep cuts spelt out the number 32.

Gary Tennant, 29 years of age, effeminate with a crown of bleached blonde hair. The locals remained calm, putting it down as a gay murder. With no obvious signs of sexual assault, assuming it to result from a lover's tiff gone wrong. The assumption sat awkwardly with Bobby Brooks, given the state of undress.

Slim in build to the point of emancipation, it didn't take a trained eye to recognise Gary Tennant as an easy target. The lack of any physical damage, other than a single stab wound to the heart and the graffiti on his chest, puzzled the Inspector.

TORMENTED

Single, unemployed, described as lonely, he lived with his widowed mother. His home, a small terraced property within yards of where his body lay. His mother, a frail woman, looking much older than her years. Her face weathered and tired, her frame small and petite. Her love for her only son, overwhelming.

She had tended to her son's every whim, pandering to his needs, beyond reproach as a mother. He, her life; all she had left since the untimely death of his father in a road accident. An ideal son, special in every way. Their relationship close and loving.

Someone needed to break the news to her. It fell to Bobby Brooks. Gladys, inconsolable, screaming, wailing, as much a victim as her son. Sedated to calm her, protect her from self-harm.

Contacted by Bobby, and the worse for wear at the time of the call, Eddie Boyle pulled himself together, gathered the tools of his trade and walked the scant distance to Vickers Street and the Tennant's home. His job to interview and give solace to Gladys.

Typical of a Castleton terrace property, its step scoured, curtains drawn in mourning across sash windows, the house appeared to be in darkness. Eddie tapped; the door opened a crack, sad, blank eyes peered out. 'Can I come in Gladys?' His voice gentle and imploring.

Once inside, Eddie noticed several photos of Gary spread across the table and floor. Baby snaps, school and holiday pics all depicting happier times. Several halves empty teacups adorned the table. An ashtray full of tab ends rested on the arm of a faux leather chair. A fire crackled in the grate, its heat filling the compact room, blackened spit marks covered the clip rug.

'Why my boy? Who would do this?' A string of questions poured from dry, chapped lips. Eddie, wanting to be anywhere but in the presence of this poor broken woman, gave no answers. Hungover, head throbbing, he wanted to get this over. Get away from the scene. The emotion-charged woman, the picture of utter despair that faced with.

'We want to run a piece on your son, the person, the senselessness of his............' 'Murder, that's the word you're looking for, murder.' She twisted a handkerchief in her hands. In an obvious state of shock, Gladys portrayed her son as one who rarely went out. 'My boy preferred to stay with me, we played cards. He was very protective and loving.' The terror of losing him hanging in her words and actions.

Eddie, overcome with compassion, had an urge to hold her, tell her everything would be all right. He hesitated, telling her he would make sure the article showed her son in a good light. 'Gentle, loving, affectionate, tell them, tell them that.'

TORMENTED

She offered tea that Eddie didn't want but dare not refuse, it gave him time to take in the room. Gladys, typical of Northern people. Salt of the earth would give you anything but cross them at your own risk. Eddie, careful, at such a sad time, not to offend her at any cost.

Central to the wall above the fireplace hung a large cross. An aroma of polish hung in the air, filling Eddie's nostrils and making him heady. A mixture of Jack Daniels and furniture polish, not a suitable match.

The Gazette ran a full column on the story, the emphasis on a gay affair gone wrong much to Eddie's disgust. With his insistence, a further story ran depicting Gary as a dutiful son, devoted to his mother with little social life outside of the home. Little appeared in the wider press and although a full investigation was conducted, it didn't receive the attention the second murder warranted.

Gladys got the full support and prayers of the townsfolk, careful not to mention to her the whisperings of the gossips professing their theories about Gary. Rumours abounded but fizzled out as the case went dead.

Angel Boyle did not have sympathy, Gary Tennant being no different to any other man. Just as fowl in his intention as the perpetrators of her mother's attack. Just as willing to have cheap sex with Angel. If that meant using force, so be it. She despised the way her own father portrayed him. His name glorified. It was a lie; she wanted to shout it from the rooftops. She remembered his grimy hands, his smutty talk, sick jokes.

The Preparation

A lot of time and effort went into creating Angel's alter ego. Hours in the gym, hours in the library learning about her craft. Days, roaming out of town, second-hand shops, seeking the right attire. Visits to hardware stores collecting cleaning supplies. All planned not to draw attention. Everything, including her look, perfect.

Angel's height meant that she didn't need to wear high-heeled shoes. It was a task necessary for her to learn, something she found painful to achieve. With practice, however, she learned to walk in a certain way, learned to put make up on attracting a certain type. The quiet children's author became the avenging angel more than she cared to admit.

Kick boxing and self-defence classes were a regular part of the preparation, Angel excelled at both. She needed to be strong, agile, prepared to fight if needed. Carrie would approve. It pleased her. The transformation didn't please her father, amazement, his reaction the first time he experienced her alter ego.

She needed to test the effectiveness of her unfamiliar look, so dropped in on Eddie. Angel delighted in his response, but not at her father's appearance. Startled at the gaunt, unkempt man standing before her, her heart told her to hug him. Her mind contradicted it.

Eddie looked weak. His eyes lifeless. He stank of booze. The entire room stank of booze. 'What happening to us mum?' Eddie failed to hear the whispered comment. Failed to see the pain in his daughter's eyes.

'What happened to mum? I want detail, please. I need you to tell me why you didn't call me, I would have come, I would have been here.' The urgency in Angel's voice quietened any protests Eddie would make.

Detail an obsession. Her father, the only one in a position to fill in the missing gaps. Why did her mother kill herself, why such a brutal method? Her mother, frail following the attack, didn't explain how she could hammer a large hook into a door, tie a knot in a thick rope, put her head in a noose and kick away the chair.

Something odd, it didn't ring true and left Angel puzzled. Her mother wouldn't take such an action. There was more to it, the only person aware of the answer, stood before her.

TORMENTED

He spoke, choosing his words, the pain of recall etched on his face. She wanted to look him in the eye, watch his reactions, signs of inconsistences, but glanced towards the closed door of the bedroom. The same door that haunted her at night, creaked open in the darkness, displayed its grotesque secret. A vision so vivid, Angel perceived the terror her mother must have experienced.

Eddie Boyle grimaced. He began, 'We wanted to protect you, both of us. Keep you safe. We thought we'd cope. She.... she said it would be okay. I thought things would be okay. Angel look at me, please. I'm so, so sorry, I didn't understand how much suffering she experienced. I'm suffering, I'd change places now if it were possible.'

Anger boiled up in Angel. She pinched her leg, hard, squeezing. She needed to remain calm, needed to bring herself down, find the release. It came, as her nail dug deep into her flesh. She bled, nodded to her father to continue.

'They dirtied her, defiled her. They ripped away her dignity, her feelings, her soul. I tried to comfort her, hold her, touch her. She hated touching. Broke every mirror in the house, didn't want to look at her body. Your mother, soiled, used. She wanted to die. Be free again, not allow anyone to see the scars. The pride she took in her appearance disappeared. I tried, I tried so much, but. It did nothing to console her.'

Angel, now slumped in her mother's chair, clenched her fist. She wanted to scream, to scream so that birds would fall from the sky. Windows would crack and disintegrate. Scream so her lungs would burst.

'Stop your hand is bleeding'. Eddie made a move towards his daughter. Angel recoiled, halting him in his tracks. He disappeared out of the room, returning several minutes later with a plaster. Without speaking she held out her hand, allowing him to place the dressing over the reddened nail tracks.

'She wouldn't leave the house. The doctor come to her, we got counsellors, did everything. The nights, the darkness, the worst. She would wake up screaming, clawing at the air. Then she would wake, sit there, bolt upright in bed, say nothing, just stare in front of her for hours and hours.'

Angel, now taking in deep breaths, held back her emotions, calming herself, eyes closed. 'Continue!' she demanded.

'She took so much medication, she became like a zombie during the day'. Her eyes appeared dead; the life sapped from them. I should have let them take her, they wanted to. Selfish, but I thought I was helping her. Angel, I didn't. I failed her, failed her.'
'I may have helped her; you didn't give me the chance.' Spat Angel. Eddie bowed his head. Defeated. Lost. Unable to keep his feelings anymore, he began

shaking, tears rolling from his eyes. A sobbing wreck that melt the hardest heart. It didn't melt his daughters.

By the time she reached her apartment, her legs, heavy and tired, sore. The gym workout hard. In a heightened emotional state following her conversation with her father. The running machine pounded harder than usual.

'There is something about running water that is relaxing', thought Angel as she poured in more bath salts, mixed them in with her uninjured hand she slid into the warmth. Down she sank, submersing the whole of her body. Good, soothing. Her eyes closed; she allowed her mind to rest.

The Return

A wide smile spread across Eddie's face as his daughter entered the room. He reciprocated. She noticed her father was clean and had shaven. Gaining weight, he looked almost healthy again.

Now, almost three months since their talk, she visited every week. Observed her father improve at each visit. She was proud of him. Today, the best in a long time. No longer shaking in need of alcohol, the sweating stopped, he resembled a human being again.

Her eyes glancing around the apartment showed that attempts to clean had taken place. Clean bedding replaced the soiled sheets, pots stood washed, windows cleaned. Eddie, still sleeping in the lounge, had grown closer to Angel. Now able to deal with the pain he carried, in a more positive way. Pleased they had talked, he had opened up, cleansed himself.

TORMENTED

No longer so alone, so isolated. He sensed a change towards him, Angel seemed to be coming to terms with her mother's death, warming, not so bitter. Eddie recognised it would take a long time to repair the relationship with his daughter, but still grateful he embraced the slight step forward. The dialogue with his daughter was open. It gave him renewed hope.

Angel showed a strength not seen in many people. As a reporter he read most people with no real effort, not so with his daughter. Her eyes hid her genuine emotions. Capable of showing him a softer side, yet capable of changing within an instance to the icy glare that almost scared him. The glare that left him puzzled, wanting, fearing.

'You look well, trying, I can tell. It's good.'

The words held great meaning to Eddie, but his response surprised her.

'It sounds daft, even morbid. I have a purpose. I am needed, I'm working on the murder cases, being asked to help by Inspector Brooks. Find out about the victims, their lives. Look for any motives, it's kind of given me fresh life.'

Angel, alert, found her father's words strange but reassuring. He welcomed getting involved; this would serve her needs. She saw by her father's expression that he relished working with the police again.'

'I need to understand the person capable of this. Commit atrocities with no apparent reason. I need to discover what the numbers mean, why they were carved into their chests. The lack of clues bothers me, can you see that?'.

She saw what he meant. This was about to become the best cat-and-mouse game she had played and with her own father. The prospect appealed to her.

'Have they found links between the bodies. Any idea of the significance of the numbers?'

Angel, now in her element, talking about her dominant interest in life, getting first-hand reports. No murderer had such a benefit This was a chase she'd enjoy.

'It's the same person, the MO is the same, but they can't find a link between the men, different ages, lifestyles, habits. No reasoning behind it. It's a mystery. I mean 32, what the hell does that mean?'

Eddie, back to the old reporter, keen, questioning, determined. Excited to be back on the job in its fullest sense. Filled with adrenalin, notebooks strewn across the table, a pencil behind his ear as Angel always remembered it. She smiled a wry smile; vengeance was being done.

Let's have a cuppa, look at the clues, see if I can help you with it.' There were no truer words spoken, how much she will help him, a different matter. Eddie would never know that.

The two cracked pots of muddy looking tea sat on the table; Eddie apologised for spilling the drink. She turned down the plate of digestives Eddie pushed towards her; Angel noticed the pile of cuttings on the floor by the chair in which she sat. She picked several up and looked at the notes filled with her father's scribble.

Eddie smiled at his daughter, thrilled at her interest in him. Eager for her to help with his research, wanting to be part of his world again. A relief, a long time coming, Eddie would grasp it.

In contrast to her father's thoughts, Angel played her game. His renewed enthusiasm she saw to be ironic. The vicious events that took her mother now bringing her father back from the brink. It gave her some satisfaction, just a little, but it came nowhere to that she would gain from avenging her mother.

She swallowed the lasts dregs of tea, then suggested cleaning the entire apartment, even the possibility of her father moving back into his own room, the marital room. The latter brought immediate angst to Eddie.

'Bit by bit, eh love? Leave the bedroom, another time.'

She smiled, she understood, opening the door repelling her as much as her father. For the rest of the day, the two cleaned, polished and sprayed, including her 'stuck in time' bedroom. By the time Angel now ready to leave, pleased at the shared jokes. They had laughed together and almost hugged at one stage.

'If you can't go back to your bedroom dad why don't you move into mine?'

A solemn look crossed Eddie's face. His recall of the last time his daughter referred to him as dad cloudy. It moved him. Holding back tears he gave a brief laugh. 'Your mum would never forgive me if I touched your room, let alone move into it.'

Angel grinned a wide grin. She wanted to bring back the lightness shared moments before. Nodding, she raised her eyes up towards the ceiling. Her room to be sacred to her mother. She had refused to let her grow up and never admitted she had grown up even when she left home.

'I need to make a move before it gets dark. It's been an excellent day'. On her next visit, they would face their fears.

The park appeared still. The user's bench empty, a dirty needle discarded next to the bin. Two joggers ran past, chattering, paying no attention to her. No one else was around. The night drawing in, dusky, dry. Shadows of trees cast fearsome images across her pathway.

TORMENTED

Angel always amused by the stark atmospheric contrast between night and day.

She walked, alert, her eyes scanning all around her. The path smooth, well-trodden, dangerous in wet weather. Her thoughts turned to the day spent with her father, she mused at the change in him. Mulled over the methods he used to uncover clues, go beyond the surface of any cases he reported on.

Relief nestled in the pit of her stomach; her relationship with her father, never seen as some would term. Now, the only relative left. She didn't want to lose him. Losing her mother affecting both in peculiar ways. Now he would help her put things right.

With that thought, her mother came rushing back into her conscious. She grimaced but fought hard not to lose the positivity of the day. Angel battled to cast out the images creeping over her mind. Anger rushed through her as she failed to stop the rising feelings of hatred, interfering with the pleasant memories she wanted to keep.

She clenched her fists, her nails dug deep into the soft flesh, squeezing she needed the release, it came but from another source. Startled by a voice that came out of nowhere, she spun around, adrenaline pumping through her body. In an instance her body was primed for action, legs in a firm stance, fists closed.

PATRICIA A SUTCLIFFE

'Hi again'. The voice sounded warm, deep, non-threatening, almost comforting, protective. Angel recognised the face from where she struggled to remember. She looked at the figure coming close to her, scanning it up and down. 'Tom, Tommo to my mates, remember me?'

Angel, now taking in all her surroundings, eyes flitting from tree to tree, shadow to shadow, aware of anyone else that might lurk around. Satisfied, her breathing slowed.

She continued her walk towards the large iron gates, now looming before her, only a short distance from the safety of her apartment. 'It's Tom, I spoke to you once before you told me your mother died.'

His comments proved enough to stop her in her tracks. She turned, faced the man keeping pace with her. Her mind flew back to the day of the funeral, back to the park bench, the stranger who thought it okay to talk to her. Bemused at the way unknowns needed to accost those who didn't give a shit about what they wanted. This annoyance, no different to her.

'Tom, you remember me!' 'I remember you'. Angel retorted, her voice crisp. 'What do you want?' The last thing she needed, to get into conversation with someone who wanted to interfere with her day.

TORMENTED

'Look, I'm not trying to come onto you. I lost my mother. It's lonely You just looked like you needed a friend.'

Taken aback at the warmth in deep brown eyes, the tenderness in his voice, she half smiled at him. Another lifetime, another day, she thought to herself, as she took in his manly looks, muscular build, dark wavy hair and a wide smile. Another time, another place maybe. Now she lacked any inclination to engage him.

Angel quickened her pace to shake off her unwanted admirer. 'Okay, I get the message, I'll just walk you to the gate, you don't want to be here after dark.' Oblivious to the icy glare given to him, he kept his pace level with hers. The gates reached, Tommo Davidson slowed down, allowing Angel to continue alone. Relieved, she crossed the road, walking a scant distance past the entrance to The Mews before turning to check he hadn't following her.

Under different circumstances his concern would have pleased her. Now, her need to get home, was all that mattered.

A voice inside grizzled away at her. Why? What had made her help her father clean his house? Why spent hours scrubbing, polishing? He deserved punishment, to suffer for his crimes. She lifted her hands to her face; the smell of disinfectant filled her senses. A pleasant odour, fresh.

Darts, how, why value a game over the safety of his wife? Why would he let her leave the pub alone? Did the moronic slime that attacked her leave the match in place of him? Who heard her screams, saw them run from the alley? They had interviewed every household overlooking the backs. It seemed impossible no one heard anything. Impossible. What were they be covering up? Perhaps one of their own did it?

Endless nights of questioning, studying, puzzling. The torment ripped at Angel's heart; nothing available to allay the visions that visited her. Played tricks with her mind in the dark, danced over rationality.

In the place she should find peace, she found none. Sleep she dreaded as much as she loathed her waking moments. The comfortable king-size bed, once nestling her deep within, as she wallowed in its security. It's soft pillows, the thick American handmade quilt, that kept her enclosed within its folds. Transformed overnight into bindings that held her down, smothered her, refused to give up its grip on her reality.

It had been a positive day. The night terrors awaiting her, never far from her, had remained hidden. 'Just one night, one night to let me sleep.' Angel forgot what deep sleep meant, the negative side of her mind refusing to release its hold on her.

Turning on the stereo, she stretched out and yawned. Soft music drifted over the room; tears streamed from

TORMENTED

Angel's eyes. They came without reason, without thoughts. She let her eyes fall closed. Her mother appeared, no smile on her face, concern in her eyes. 'I'm scared for you, Angel'.

Carrie Boyle's face bore a soft glow, her eyes tender and deep. The scars no longer there, the misshapen jawline straight again. Angel embraced the touch of her mother's hand across her brow. A contentment fell over her, her eyes closed once more.

For the first time in a long time, sleep engulfed her. Angel woke relaxed. The blue velvet bedroom curtains rose, falling, tickled by the breeze blowing through the half-opened window. Today felt good. Her thoughts drifted to Tom. She wondered about his apparent interest in her, why he seemed keen to talk to her.

Tommo Davidson

Tom Davidson, a Jack the Lad. Married young, divorced young, several live in's, now living with his pregnant partner. Attempts to lead a settled life seemed to elude him. News that he going to become a father shocked him, the thought of such a responsibility scaring him. An ability to be loyal weighing on his mind.

Appearance always a top priority to him, attracting the opposite sex a second priority. His roving eye got him into more than one scrape, but a declaration of pregnancy, his life now thrown into turmoil. At 42, he considered himself too old to think about becoming a father. What would he do now? Care for a mother and child? He didn't want to care for a mother and child. Why? He had been so stupid?

He now faced a situation hard to worm his way out of. A dilemma he would have to face, and it had a profound effect on him.

TORMENTED

He had suggested an abortion, but she wanted none of it. Now he had become well and truly trapped. Tommo didn't enjoy being trapped by a girl he lived with just a matter of months. Convinced the pregnancy, orchestrated as a scheme to hook him, it took away any acceptance by him towards her or the baby.

An only child, spoilt by his mother, idolised by his father, he wanted for nothing, including his choice of women. Things came easily to him. As a singer, in his youth he played to packed nightclubs in packed towns across the country, taken his fair share of dope, been in his fair share of fights, dismissed his fair share of blank memories.

Tommo boasted many stories, tales of irresponsible and headstrong pranks played on unsuspecting pals. Heady carefree days spent living his life. His doting parents waiting in the background should he need them.

Nowadays, his drug fuelled parties lay behind him. Now, satisfied with local gigs, small audiences and little renumeration, he missed the adoration, the freedom of the road. Above all, he missed the adoration of young fans, eager to please in any way he chose.

In his heyday he bedded girls much younger than himself, with no real thought for any hidden offspring he might have generated. Nor did he Sarah, his latest, he'd met at a gig. Different to most women he bedded, she appealed to him. Shy, withdrawn, nervous, attractive. He preferred redheads or blondes. Sarah was dark.

With the pregnancy, any physical attraction he had towards her went. Sex became something he performed as a personal necessity rather than a joint venture. Bored, he longed for the thrill of the chase again, playing 'God's waiting room' venues, offered him little chance of that.

When he met the mysterious redhead in the park, his ego convinced him that fate had taken a hand. She made his curiosity rise as fast as his ego dropped when she showed little interest in him. For Tommo, a novel experience, a challenge he determined he would win. To him, it was game on.

Rejection didn't come easy to him; he didn't like it, failed to accept it. It became a fixation with him. He would make a conquest of the strange, beguiling woman or he'd die in trying. Thoughts of lust and seduction occupied his mind. He liked the challenge it gave him, the purpose. He would thrive on the adventure.

Determined to give himself every chance, he took to hanging around the park. Hours spent on the bench by the path, idling his time, thinking how He would approach her, what he would say. His overriding obsession, now stoking up the fire within him. He would have her. Just a matter of time, he surmised.

TORMENTED

The wind, bitter, blowing in all directions, a golfer's nightmare. Trees bowed and swayed under the power of the gusts. Leaves flittered, hopping across the ground, rising and falling, some refusing to be ripped from their branches.

An old couple struggled hard to walk against its force. It pushed them forward at a pace faster than their frail bodies moved. They clung to each other for support, heads down, collars pulled high. On they struggled, until, exhausted, they sought shelter in the bandstand.

Paper made its escape from an overturned bin, chased by a dog who grasped a chance at freedom, its lead still attached, bouncing up and down as it ran. An exasperated owner shouted commands and tried in vain to catch his beloved pet.

No kind of day to sit in the park but Tom Davidson had no intention of letting that deter him his mission. Wrapped in an oversized parka, the hood pulled over his head. A shudder ran through him as the relentless wind blasted at his body. He shuddered again; he would give it another ten minutes then go to the Moon for a pint.

The thought made him smile. Nothing beat sitting before an open fire sipping a cold pint. Soon he would chat with his mates, several of which would have been there for several hours. They would be at their regular table, playing cards, laughing at smutty jokes, his chair empty, waiting for him.

Tom stood up. In the distance he recognised the jogging figure. His heart did a flip as the tall, slender, red-haired runner came nearer. Her hair blew in the wind, whipping across her face. It created an image of flames dancing around her head, warming up the bitter day.

The sight of Tom didn't warm up Angel. She stopped, rested her hands of her knees and caught her breath. She contemplated turning, jogging around the park, but why should she? Why think about him, she could ignore him? An array of solutions floated across her mind. Rational Angel would carry on, ignore him. Emotional Angel wondered why she thought of him at all.

'Hi there.' Tom grinned, his brown eyes twinkling. Much as she didn't want it to, her heart jumped at the realisation he may wait there for her. Stalker came to mind. Tom saw the puzzlement on her face.

Annoyed at his persistence, she challenged him. 'What the fuck's wrong with you? Are you some stalker, make it a habit of accosting women, do you?' He cut in. 'Just trying to be friendly, didn't think it a crime.' His smile broad, his face red, the wind biting, whistling around them.

TORMENTED

Angel faced her foe; he faced his prey. 'You're shivering, take my coat'. Displeasure spread across her face; she didn't want nor to need his concern. Angel looked at him, an unpleasant look. He removed his coat from her shoulders and apologised. She recoiled, startled by her reaction. He stepped back.

Angel studied his flushed face; he was pleasant to look at? Her gaze unflinching, her eyes penetrating, watching his every movement, she reddened.

.

'Meet me at the gates in 30 minutes, we'll go for a coffee.' Taken aback by the demanding sound in her voice, all he muttered and nodded in agreement.

'What the hell are you doing, idiot?' 'What are you thinking?' Angel reproached herself. Her gut told her she was making a definite wrong move, but something about the man took away all rationale. He annoyed her to a fault, he pestered her. His actions appeared creepy, but something stopped her from rejecting him outright.

The 'Pantry', a well-used, posh little café on Castleton High Street, was homely. Checked blue tablecloths adorned small square tables, in their centre a vase of silk bluebells. The décor reeked of warmth; the air hung with an infusion of ground coffee. A safe place, one that Angel would never frequent. Chosen for that reason. She wanted to keep Tom separate from her general routine, a key element in her choice of coffee house.

His hands shook as he set the two cappuccinos down, the cups clinking. A little spilt on the pristine cloth, much to Tom's embarrassment. She enjoyed his awkwardness, prolonging the silence. Her voice warmer when she spoke, but far from friendly.

'Okay, we're here, what do you want from me and why do you keep accosting me?' Her questions blunt, Tom became unnerved. This situation was new to him, one he was unfamiliar with; he didn't understand it and didn't enjoy. Tommo like to be in control in opposite-sex relationships. The aggressor when getting rid of an unwanted conquest.

Bags sat propped up by the side of chairs, shopping spilling out. Clanking of cups surrounded them, idle chit chat from windswept patrons pleased at the respite of a warm cuppa.

Tom noted Angel's critical gaze. It pierced at his soul. Forced to look away, he became tense, unsure of himself. 'Well! You have me at your mercy, I asked you why you are harassing me?' Sensing an interrogation taking place, he blurted out a stunted apology. 'I wanted to talk to you, that's all. I don't have any ulterior motives.' He lied, wanting to disappear beneath the seat.

His bewildered expression amused her; Angel smiled for the first time. Did she want to give him a chance?

TORMENTED

Did she need this distraction? Under normal circumstances she may give him the benefit of the doubt. Now, the thought of anything stopping her achieving her goal made her balk. Held her back, refused to let her become entangled.

She turned down his offer of friendship. The rejection stung at him. He gulped down the remnants of the remaining coffee and stood to leave. Angel thanked him for his time. Angered at the callousness of her comment, he retorted. 'You invited me; I didn't understand it was fucking interview.'

THE AWAKENING

Eddie sat, his hand on his temple. The mother of all headaches throbbing in his head. Sober for over a month, his body still suffered withdrawal symptoms. He'd gone from being pissed up every night to just two pints. Not the best way to return to sobriety. Eddie, aware of how hard his task was, considered this to be the only way to achieve it. Clear of the numbness that attaches itself to alcohol, reality had set in.

2.30pm, Angel would arrive soon, an event Eddie always thrived on, not today. Today he dreads the visit. Wished the promises were reversible. He wanted to carry on through, honour the plan. Clear Carrie's room. A task he would do anything to avoid. The room remained like a mausoleum, untouched since her death.

TORMENTED

Eddie's senses may return to normal but emotionally he remained far from strong. The support of Angel would be crucial, with her he would face the inevitable.

'We have to go in dad, have to go in now.' There would be pain opening the door. Eddie made excuses to get cleaning materials and disappeared into the kitchen, Angel closed her eyes and sighed. Two hours lapsed since she entered the apartment. General talk now exhausted, probing questions about her lifestyle, avoided. The time had come.

A chill ran through her body. The door had long since become a barrier, now it stood ajar. She entered, pulling Eddie with her. They stood, the chalk mark on the floor fading, her father's eyes etched with pain. 'We can do this.' Her voice firm and decisive. An odour of death hung in the air. The room cold, still, Angel threw open the curtains. Grabbed the bucket from her father's hands. 'Leave it to me dad. Go into the lounge, NOW!' his daughter commanded. He obeyed.

She set to scrubbing the floor, aware of her knuckles scraping the surface but knowing the pain needed to keep her anger in control. Dust filled on her mouth, she shouted to her father to make tea. No longer did her mother's scent linger, now long gone. Devoid of soul, the décor dated and tired.

From her kneeling position, the figure of her father, cup in hand, filled her with longing of what she had lost. 'Help me get the bedding off.' The softness in her voice, new to Eddie. He placed his arm around her shoulder, bowed this head, cried. They said nothing, words unnecessary. She stood, hugged him and wiped his tears. The two people who loved Carrie Boyle most, came together united in grief.

Angel's eyes rested on the dressing table; her mother's pure bristle hairbrush still lay there. By its side, a small silver powder compact. She pulled the brush through her own hair, her mind flicked back to the many times Carrie brushed her hair. The strokes, massaging her scalp, she closed her eyes. She was with her mother.

Her father's voice broke into her thoughts. 'I still think of her, still talk to her. Didn't think she would do it; I'll never forgive myself, never.'

Alerted to his words, puzzled, Angel turned. Eddie now perched on the edge of the bed, his voice a whisper, faltering but audible enough for her to drop the brush. His comments troubled her, changing her mood.

Eye contact avoided, she wiped the furniture over with a damp cloth, working in silence until the room came alive. Her final task, to make the bed up. 'You'll move back in here tonight?' She half questioned; half demanded. Eddie nodded, to face his demons would be a start.

TORMENTED

With the air between them tense, they moved into the lounge. 'What did you mean you didn't think she would do it?' Eddie shuffled; she wouldn't let his comments go by without a full explanation.

Scared to lose any progress made with her, he hesitated. Got himself a glass of water and sat down facing her. Afraid to lose the trust he had seen returning, he chose his words. His daughter would understand, he must be straight with her.

Eddie longed for a drink, anything to get him through the next hour. He paused, gulped at the water. A tremor ran through him, his voice trembled, his words reluctant. 'You can't realise how depressed your mother got. In pain, unable to sleep even with medication. She begged me to end her misery'.

Angel sat in silence; her lips closed. Her breathing rapid. Eddie continued. 'She had no escape left for her, nightmares filled, and dark visions tormented her. Scared to go out, scared to stay in. A prisoner without hope of release. She prayed for an end, convinced they would seek her out. Finish the job.

Hair now in a tight knot, Angel pulled it hard. 'Stop it, stop.' Eddie cried out in alarm. Angel looked at what was now a shadow of her father. Unable to stop herself, she clung to the dejected man crumpled before her.

'I'm sorry Angel, so sorry. I was lost, struggling. She just gave up; her mind destroyed. No amount of counselling, treatments, psychiatrists helped. She turned her back on the World. What was left of her, she was no more than an empty shell.'

'What did you do dad?' Angel sounded tired, beaten.

'I pushed her to come with me. Fucking dart match. It didn't matter. A before her safety. I bought the tablets; I should never have bought the tablets.' His voice a whisper, his sense of relief great, his secret now released.

His actions that had tortured him for three years since Carrie's suicide, now out in the open. He had spoken to someone he trusted. A weight lifted from him, a burden laboured with, exorcised.

Angel urged him to continue. She needed to understand the extent to which her father helped her mother end her life. Her arms still around him, Eddie Boyle failed to see the rapid change in his daughter's demeanour. Back, the icy glare of her eyes. His sentences now shorter, almost spat out, he continued.

'She begged me, down on her knees, pleading with me. Her headaches always there, they never stopped. How could I just stand by, see her suffer day after day?' Overcome with emotion Eddie, he fixed his eyes on

Angel. He hoped for a sign of compassion. There was none.

Angel stared at the pitiful man, full of guilt, remorseful. The man who was telling her how he helped kill her own mother. 'Continue.' Her voice tone unnerved him. He pleaded with her to understand. Told her of the vast amount of strong medication she took to survive each day. 'She was like a zombie, moving, room to room in a stupor. I folded; it was too much to bear.'

'Did you put the hook in the doorframe?' The question direct, demanding. Eddie's head bowed; nodded an affirmative. Angel let out a loud gasp. Shaking, fighting to control herself. 'They destroyed you both, didn't they?' He had no response, she no need of one.

'Were you there when it happened when she did it?' Eddie, broken, exclaimed, 'No' his voice loud and imploring. 'How can you think that I'm not a fucking monster?' It was the first time he had raised his voice during the conversation.

She shifted her gaze. Her response, here, now, could destroy or save her father. She tried to re-focus, come to terms with information she had pushed for but never wanted. Was her father a murderer?

He had made progress, been trying to get his life back. Life with her mother had to have been poor, soul destroying. Had he not hugged at her mother's pillow, refusing to let go? Had she ever doubted the love they had for each other?

Angel knew how deep their feelings went. How they were always together, never going out without each other. Supporting each other through everything life threw at them.

She held her arms out, Eddie moved to hug his daughter. Together they sobbed. Tension faded away in an instance. They now had each other.

'Tell me the rest dad, finish this.' Her tone warm, soft, encouraging. 'She asked me to put a hook up, weeks before she..........' His voice trailed off. 'She believed they were out to get her, wanted to hang something on the door, know if it opened. That was the one she wanted, I daren't challenge her. Her mind was too fragile. I complied with all she said, all she asked of me. She was near the edge, one refusal she would tip over.'

Angel stopped him. He had suffered enough. Pushing her finger from his lip, he continued. 'She was tired that day, told me to go for a drink, took her sleeping tablets, went to bed. I thought a quick drink, no harm in it. She assured me, pushed me to go. I had one pint; I swear. It was one pint too many, I got back too late.'

Angel kissed her father's forehead. All burdens lifted, he felt relief wash over him. 'It's getting dark dad; I have to go. I have work to do.' Tonight, she would vent the rage and anger in her body.

PATRICIA A SUTCLIFFE

A Push Too Far

The green contact lens in Angel placed the brown ones back in their container. Tonight, was different. Her hair hung down her back in a ponytail. It would be covered by the wig. Cherry lipstick caressed her mouth, she smoothed it out with her little finger. Eye shadow and black liner completed the look. Her working clothes, laundered, remained the same.

She checked her bag. Packed all the equipment. The hidden pocket in her jacket housed her knife. Placed perfectly. She'd draw it, swiftly, when the time came.

Baker Street was like no other. Interwoven with alleyways running its full length, meshing to form a common identity. At each corner, top and bottom, stood lamps. Dirty with neglect, they gave little light out, leaving the alleys dimly lit.

This was a rundown, a dilapidated area of Town badly in need of a facelift. Each alleyway, known as backs to the locals, housed the gates of the rows of terraced properties making up the streets.

As a child Angel spent long hours playing in these streets. Enjoyed the safety they held for her. Mothers in the close-knit community, watching from the windows as children ran up and down, kicking cans, throwing balls.

Daylight hours were much the same today. Streets a hive of activity. Protective parents doing the school run. Local buses filled with shoppers. Gates cracked under the weight of women as they leant over them gossiping. Cheerful places filled with laughter and the noise of living.

At night they took on a unique aura. Dark and foreboding. Where secret lovers met, hidden from sight. Local youths hung out; their shadowy forms, highlighted beneath the glow of the lamps. Cheap cider cans lay discarded amongst the tab ends and odd syringe.

Angel loathed the louts who littered her childhood memories. Unemployed yobs with no regard for residents. Smoking and drinking little, she saw them as wasters, living off the earnings of those choosing to work.

Still early, Angel entered the Moon. Heads turned; heads always turned when she dressed this way. The snug clientele whispered. Bar props passed smutty remarks. This was the attention she wanted, worked hard for.

The resemblance she bore to her mother went unnoticed. How quickly they had forgotten her. The clothes she wore, the gestures she made.

Emerald green eyes moved from face to face. She rested on no one specific. 'Gin and Tonic.' She ordered her mother's tipple. She longed for the guilty, tormented by their nightmares, to come forward. They never did.

She moved against the bar; her right foot perched on the foot rail. 'God, I know why you didn't want to entertain me. I forgot to offer you fucking money.' She knew the voice. Enraged, she downed her drink, spun on her heels and left the bar.

Tommo, determined not to let his prey get away, followed. 'Come on, I was joking.' She was furious, aborting her mission now, the only option left to her. A waste of preparation time, the psyching up she had done. Angel hated to waste her time.

'What's with the fucking wig?' Intoxicated, he hadn't noticed the change in eye colour. Tommo reached for her arm. The dangerous path he was about to take unknown to him. 'Can't you take a joke.' Angel stopped dead in her tracks. Faced him head on. 'Fuck off, I just want to go home, okay?' Her words were stressed.

Beer befuddling his senses, he attempted again to put his arm around her. She pulled away. Undeterred, he tried to kiss her. She spat; it would turn nasty sooner than she wanted. Unsure which way to take it, she pushed him. He fell, too unsteady on his feet to remain upright. His head cracked on the pavement.

His protests ignored, he staggered to his feet. 'Let me go on my way Tommy.' Incensed, her lack of concern angering him, he retaliated.' Tommo, Tommo, silly bitch. Is it so hard to remember my name?

'GO AWAY.' The harshness in her voice a warning. A warning he failed to take. Only one way would this end. Aware of his youth and strength, she had to take advantage of the drink in his system.

'Let's go to the Park.' Her voice was clinical, measured. Her wits alert and keen. The street was too public, too near the Moon. Too risky to work in. The walk she didn't relish. It was a necessity. Head down, she began to move forward.

Darkness enveloped the park. The dealers long gone. A cold chill hung in the air as they entered the gates from the Town end. Stumbling, the effects of alcohol taking hold, Tom held onto Angel's arm for balance.

Alert, aware of her surroundings, she walked in silence. She didn't want this, didn't like this, but had no choice. It may go wrong. She wasn't in charge of the situation. The person before her had pursued her, invaded her personal space. It had to end.

Tommo steered Angel towards a clump of dense trees, standing to the far side of the path. Half pushing, half directing, her choices being limited. It was time to act, take control. 'Further in Tom, move further in.' The obvious pleasure at her suggestion spread across his face.

Now he groped her. Hands running down her hair and back settled on her backside. His face too close to hers, she allowed him to kiss her. She smelt the strong aftershave he was wearing. An unattractive smell, cheap and nasty, mixed with the tang of beer. Equally cheap and nasty.

Her senses keen, Angel became aware of footsteps on the path. Tommo, unaware, his full concentration on her, continued his fondling. Now uncomfortable, she tried to pull away. He was having none of it.

Witnesses were something she could not afford. There had to be no mistakes. Now was the time to call it a day, leave. It was too risky; she had to leave.

TORMENTED

Tommo had different ideas. He had his mind set on other things. Leaving wasn't one of them. He panted hard, his hands squeezing and grabbing at her body. Angel's head was whirling. She tried to reason, take stock of her situation. 'Look, I like you, but I don't want this now. I want to go home.'

A wide grin across his face masked the determination in his eyes. 'Come on gorgeous, we both want the same. Stop fucking me about.' He was strong than she thought. Now becoming aggressive, one hand pushing up her dress, the other holding her. Pinning her to the tree.

She had to keep calm. Inside, she felt anything but. Busy with his attempts to kiss her again, he failed to notice her slip as she slipped her hand inside of her coat. The first he knew was the thud, followed by a searing pain. He staggered backwards, clutching his chest. Thoughts of lust replaced by the fear now gripping him.

Anger and surprise overcame him. He lunged forward, grabbing at her. The second thud came. He was stronger than she thought. Tom slid down onto his hands, his knees buckling beneath him. He dropped backwards onto the trodden grass, his eyes wide and staring. Angel was shaking, a slight panic growing within her. This was a new situation, a dangerous situation.

PATRICIA A SUTCLIFFE

Her task was completed, but the body lay in sight of the path. Seen by anyone who ventured down the path. Her watch read 11.30pm. the pubs and clubs would let out. Guaranteed, the revellers would enter the park, the same thing on their minds as Tom Davidson.

To move him would take time. Time, she hadn't got. A deep red stain spread across the white fur of her jacket. She dragged him, covered in blood, far enough into the trees, hidden from sight.

Her knife now an instrument, she worked skilfully, with precision. The number 32 etched into his chest. Her work completed she packed her bag being sure the check the contents were as they be. Sprinted to the opposite side of the path. She saw no one and felt relief.

The large bag lay on the floor, zipper open and contents in view. She took out the plastic carrier, removed her outer clothing, pushed it into the bag along with her heels. Dragged the black tracksuit over her cold body.

Adrenaline pumped through her veins. Her heart was pumping faster than normal. She checked the ground. She'd left nothing behind. Then, breaking into a jog, she raced for the park gates and home.

Furious, wanting to scream, she slammed the bag to the floor. 'All he had to do, take no for a fucking answer.

TORMENTED

Leave me alone. Stupid prick.' Her fist banged hard into her chest, it hurt, she wanted it to.

Her task complete, she had been messy. Caught off guard, emotion had. got in the way. Weeks of preparation wasted. Thoughts of failure angered her. He wasn't the victim she chose; he chose himself. Took control away. Now she had to settle down, calm her mind.

Routine was vital, well-practised, almost mechanical. Washing machine whirring. Stained work wear cleansed. All evidence removed. Next, she scraped her heels, removing the grass residue, dried blood and mud. All done, bath run. The aroma of oils filled her senses, a welcome relief dispersing the heady aftershave of Tom Davidson.

Face beneath the surface, she held her breath. Counted the seconds. Steamy water caressed her. Relaxed, peaceful, her body rose from the water. A large scratch across her chest stung with the coldness of the air. Angel cursed. 'Stupid bastard. How?' It was clear how Tommo had lunged at her in panic when the knife hit its mark for the first time.

It would be covered on her next visit to her father. The last thing she needed was interrogating.

Tired, body aching, muscles sore from dragging a heavy body, sleep beckoned.

Sarah's Story

Tommo was late home. Used as Sarah was to his habits, it annoyed her. Sick of being alone, her boyfriend drinking any money they had down the drain.

Young, pregnant and confused. Her hands rubbed the unwelcomed lump. Her flat stomach a thing of the past. What the future would bring troubled her. Did he love her, want the baby? Did she even trust him? He had a chequered past. Had he changed? Promises he made with ease. Breaking them even easier for him.

News of the pregnancy had shocked them both. Was he pleased he said he was? Talked about 'his son', thought about names. Made plans, painted the old drawers blue. It would be fine. She was panicking.

When the spotlight landed on her, she had become embarrassed. Gone red, cringed. Was he singing for her? Plain, mousy Sarah. Everyone in the club eyed her. All she wanted was the ground to open, swallow her.

Sarah, too shy to look at the handsome singer, squirmed as he approached, kissed her hand and continued to sing. Tommo knew the effect of his charm on the ladies, wallowed in it. Sarah would be easy prey.

Dainty, demure. A novelty to him. He would enjoy the challenge. Weeks later Sarah, unpacked her small brown case, moved in and settled into the life of a domestic.

Overjoyed, her soulmate by her side, life was good. Things changed. A child on the way, Tommo preferred the pub to home. The small terrace now, her prison. In total control of the relationship, the man she adored came and went as he pleased.

Midnight had come and gone. Sarah worried. 12.50 pm, no sign of her man. Worried, his cell unanswered, panic was setting in. Several times, it sang out, no answer. Police sirens pierced the silence. In the street's darkness, visibility was low. Their child, due in three months, kicked. Where was he? She needed him. How would she cope if he had left her?

More sirens rang out into the night. Sarah's heart raced. Scared at the feeling in the pit of her stomach. Her mind moved from scenario to scenario. Most of them not good. With every sound of a car, her heart lifted only to be disappointed.

1.45 am still no sign. Something was wrong. Emotions ran high. In desperation she dialled 999. 'Emergency, how can I help?' The stern voice shocked her. Anxious, Sarah blurted out her story. Informed to report it again after 24 hours left her uncertain.

The kicks were stronger, niggling pains starting in her groin. Clasping her hands to her swollen abdomen, she cried. Something was wrong. She knew it.

Pacing the room, clock watching, scared the baby would arrive so early. What could she do? The pains were now becoming more severe. Again, she tapped 999. 'Emergency, how can I help you?' 'Ambulance please, I think something's wrong, I'm pregnant. I'm worried it's not due yet.' Fifteen minutes later Sarah was in a hospital bed.

Excuses wouldn't put this one right. She wanted him here, right now. His child was about to be born. Determined to stand no nonsense, he would end his escapades now or face the consequences. She would be cool. Not show him it mattered.

Another pain removed her bravado. Please let him be okay, I can't do this alone. Let him be all right. A nurse's voice cut into her thoughts. 'A false alarm. We're letting you go home. To be as stressed as this isn't good for the baby.'

Curtains pulled back; Sarah looked out of the window. A black car drew up. The doors swung open. 'He wouldn't dare bring someone back here. He just wouldn't dare.' Sarah's voice was firm. A loud knock on the door stopped her in her tracks.

A chill ran through her. She shook. She called out. 'Police miss, please open the door.' Two officers, solemn faced, entered the room. 'Sit, please.' Sarah obeyed, heart racing. The female officer spoke, firmly. 'Is it Tom?' heads nodded.

Her mind numb, she lurched forward, her face banged onto the coffee table. Instantly the policewoman was by her side. She took the brunt of the fall. Coming round, Sarah put her hand to her stomach. 'My baby, something's wrong.'

MO Profiling

'**Serial killer loose in Castleton**.' Residents spooked at the headlines, demanded answers. Truths and untruths were rife. Everyone thought they knew the victim, speculated the murderer.

Angel read paper to paper, bemused. Then, one headline sent shivers down her spine. '**Grieving girlfriend loses partner and baby to murderer.** 'Stunned to the core. Angel read and re-read the article. 'Bastard. Girlfriend. Baby'. Blood boiling, thoughts that Tom Davidson's death was a mistake, gone in an instance. He deserved to be dead. The baby did not. Sickened, she wanted to see Sarah, tell her what her boyfriend was like. Say of her sorrow at the loss of her child. How much she wanted to do that. It would never happen.

Eddie Boyle sat in his chair, head in his hands. 'Dad, you okay?' A smile crossed his face. 'Another murder.

The worst one yet.' Questions posed; Angel let her father lead the conversation. 'Did you interview this girlfriend it talks about?' Reporting the human side, his forte.

'The CID have been brought in. The fucking Town's inundated with reporters and police. All over the fucking place. Eddie was agitated. Under pressure to get his story amidst the chaos. Angel reassured him. 'You know the Town dad, the people. They trust you. If anyone can the truth out there it will be you.'

'The girlfriend, Sarah. No one has got near her. Police are protecting her. She's not local, lived here less than a year, that's all. Pregnant, she lost the baby, poor cow. Bob's organised to get her parents here.

Different this one Angel. Personal. Two murders as far as Bob is concerned.' 'I'll make tea.' Angel had to breathe. Gather her thoughts, she felt nauseous. Red welts stung her arm as her nails dug in deep. She hated herself. 'It was his fault, his. The bastard. It wasn't my fault. It wasn't.' Inside, she was screaming.

The kitchen was tidy. Green checked curtains with matching frill. Her mother had sewn them, she had helped. The heavy wooden cross brought back from the Holy Land, still hung over the table. It had been her grandmother's. A family heirloom, precious. Useless. It hadn't protected her mother from taking her own life.

PATRICIA A SUTCLIFFE

The kettle whistled. Angel prepared the thick brown teapot in the way she had been taught. 'Warm the pot with boiling water, two spoons of Yorkshire tea, always Yorkshire. Stir. Put the woolly green tea cosy over the pot.' Her mother's instructions had been precise. Ignore them at your peril.

Eddie held the cup high. Formed a circle between thumb and forefinger to tell Angel the tea was good. Together they listened to the news on the flat screen Sony. The last gift she had bought her parents the year before her mother's death.

Angel turned up the sound, what she heard sent panic through her. Witnesses had been asked to come forward. Of special interest, a woman seen to leave the Half Moon Public House at the same time as the victim.

Even more chilling, the description put out. A CID officer described the woman as tall, slender, brown hair and green eyes. Emphasising, the eyes as being striking. Wearing a tight red dress and white coat. At the end of the report it was requested that the woman come forward to be ruled out of the enquiry.

'Thank God, you've got blue eyes and red hair, Angel. I'd be turning you in.' Eddie laughed. A pallor had spread his daughter's face. 'I don't dress like a tart.' She spat. Surprised at her reaction to his joke, Eddie pointed out the officer had never said that. A stickler for detail, her father dealt with facts.

TORMENTED

Eddie Boyle hated not being in the thick of it. Trusted reporter or not, he knew he would not be interviewing Sarah any time soon. It would have to wait until the CID had done with her. His only source, police statements, same as everyone else.

Kissing her father's forehead, she made her excuses and left. Keen to be home. Tucking her long hair in the back of her coat, she headed for Town. Visits on route to several newsagents, picking up a different national in each, armed her with enough information to judge reactions to her work.

Her primary source remained the Castleton Gazette. Ever proud to read her father's articles. His intuition beyond that of a reporter's instinct. What he was thinking always important to her. What ideas did he have about the killings?' At home she could concentrate on press reports without her father seeing any signs of improper reaction.

Cordoned off by the police, the park gates hung closed. Reporters hung around everywhere. Laughing, joking. The seriousness of the crimes eluded them. To them, just business.

To circumnavigate the railings would add fifteen minutes to her time. It was bad. Through the railings, she saw officers combing the ground on their knees. A white tented area blocked any sight of the murder scene from view.

Instinct told her; they would find any clues left by her. It filled her with uncertainty. Plans had to be made.

It was now at a different level; Angel knew it. A level she wasn't happy about.

'Bobby said anything to you?' Eddie shook his head. 'I'll get nothing until he can release info. He'll need permission now. It's gone above him. Just sit back and wait.'

Goodbye said with a kiss to her father's head. Excuses made; she was on her way home. Hair tucked in the back of her coat; it would take around fifteen minutes to reach the Town.

Several newsagents were passed on her way home. From each one she bought a different newspaper. The Castleton Gazette, one of them. Angel trusted her father's articles. The gift of intuition, the norm to Eddie. It was crucial that she knew his thoughts. His ideas about the killings, clues he had.

A cordon sealed off the park. Reporters were everywhere, hanging around the gates, mingling with rubber neckers. Police officers scrutinised passers-by. To Circumnavigate the park would add fifteen minutes to her journey. It annoyed her.

A white tent was visible through the railings. On their knees, hands combing the ground, officers moved in unison searching for clues. Fear rose in Angel's throat. Plans must be made.

Stomach churning, shoes kicked off. Papers spread out on the floor; Angel settled to concentrate on each article. All carrying their own account of who, why, and how. None resembling the truth. Notes made, a glass of Chablis in hand, she flicked on the news channel.

Full of theories and scare mongering. Described as a monster, psychopath, local male who knew the area well. Responsible for killings across the country. It was clear the media profile was far off the mark. A relief, Angel smiled, their attempts at investigation pathetic.

Bored, she returned to her papers. Turned the Gazette pages. Her father's report, page 4. Low key, full of facts.

'On Saturday night another murder took place in Castleton. Police stay baffled. To date, no known link has been found between the victims. Police confirmed that the latest victim is Mr Tom Davidson, last seen leaving the Half Moon Public House. Police want to talk to a tall, slim, green-eyed woman who left the pub at the same time as the victim. You are urged to contact the information desk on Castleton 557349 if you have any information which will aid the police in their investigations.'

Angel read with interest, wondering why her father had omitted to mention the clothing. Accuracy, normally automatic to him.

Tonight, Angel would talk to her mother. She poured another large glass of wine, switched off the lights and headed to bed. She felt safe. Her mother was near. Smiling, proud. Angel knew she would be. Relaxed, the wine taking effect; she drifted in the darkness.

Radiant and childlike, she walked side by side with her mother. They were in the park, the grass greener than she remembered. Vibrancy everywhere. Heat cast out from the sun, washed over them. Warm and loved. Life was enjoyable. The two belonged together, never happier than in each other's company.

A gentle breeze caressed trees, their branches swayed as birds sang their lullabies. The look in her mother's eyes, tender, kind. Angel reached towards her. Then blackness. Thrust back into the room, the shrill ring of her mobile crashed through her dream, dragging her back to reality.

Persistent, angry ringing. The kind that says pick it up. Few people knew her number. Her publisher wouldn't ring at this hour. That left only her father. 'Yes.' Her father's voice, solemn, serious. 'They have some news about your mother's attack.' Angel, alert in an instance, grabbed her coat and ran.

TORMENTED

Bobby Brooks, true to his word, had never stopped looking for Carrie's attackers. The case always open, irrespective of other cases, including the current murders. It was a promise he had made to Carrie at her bedside. A promise he would never break.

Angel jogged the couple of miles to the apartment. Arriving out of breath, she ran up the steps. Eddie waited, tea mashing in the pot. The door left open for his daughter. 'Well, what news.' Wide eyed she listened as Eddie, excited, told her a DNA swab taken from Carrie had scored a match.

Unable to take in what she heard; Angel dropped into a chair. 'A man arrested, drunk and disorderly. They took a sample. Ran it through the database as they always do. It came back a match. Bob is interviewing him now.'

'Fuck, I can't believe it. I can't believe it, dad. All this time. Who is he? Where does he live? Who were the others?' Eddie held up his hand. 'Slow down, I've told you as much as I know. We must wait now, pray the bastard admits the attack. Gives the names of the rest.'

Eddie was coming to terms with Carrie's death. He had stopped his binges, smartened himself up. With a conviction, the healing process could begin. He poured the tea, thankful that the tragedy endured by them both hadn't destroyed his daughter as it had him.

Her mind whirling, the faces of the men she had murdered swimming in head, Angel tried to focus. The news both lifted her and brought fear to her. 'They tried to do the same to me. Would have raped me. They deserved to pay for that.' Desperately, she wanted to justify her reign of terror.

'Did Inspector Brooks say anything else to you?' He rolled his eyes to the ceiling. Half smiled. Impatient, she stared at him. 'Well, dad'.' Eddie could see his reflection in her deepness of her eyes. Crystal clear, like Carrie's. 'You are so like your mother, same smile, same eyes, same impatience.'

Eddie had been told more, but not about Carrie. 'It's about the killings. It baffles even the top notches. No motive fits. 32 means nothing, just a number. It makes little sense. What man kills without motive? No signs of sexual activity, yet the victims were all in a state of undress.'

'Perhaps he just hates drunks.' Eddie grinned at his daughter's statement. 'Perhaps. Bob thinks they may get some leads from the last one. Several witnesses have come forward. They need to find this woman; she could tell them where he went after he left her. If anyone else was with them.'

'How do they know for certain he was with a woman?'

'Several witnesses saw him with a tall brown-haired woman in the Town. No one knows who she is though.'

The recall ability of the public had always fascinated angel. The drunks who saw only what they fantasised they saw. She recalled her father's London days. The jokes he told. Descriptions given by victims of crime. His way of laughing, describing his interviewees as having the memories of schizophrenics. According to the British public, every person had many faces, voices and characters.

Eddie continued to explain to Angel how no stone was being left unturned. They were waiting for the autopsy results. 'Bob is convinced the killer will strike again if not caught. Time is critical now.'

This was the Eddie of old talking. The reporter with the bit between his teeth. Inside, she was at odds with herself but pleased at the return of her father. Also relieved, they were seeking a male. What she would do next, she didn't know.

Paul Fowler

Sat, shoulders bent forward, head in hands. Paul Fowler was not pleasant to see. A drunk, alleged paedophile and wife beater, he was a frequent sight in the pubs around Town.

Slight in stature, he stank of body odour. A pock-marked face and brown stained teeth completed the picture. Diagnosed with liver damage. He cared about no one, including himself.

Bitter accusations of assaults on children making him a marked man. His story was typical. Aged 58, wife long gone, taking the children with her. Sick of his abuse. Alcohol now his companion.

'I'll ask you again. How can you account for your DNA being found on the clothing of Carrie Boyle?'

Bobby Brooks towered over the shrivelled body of Paul Fowler. He continued to press the captive. 'Who were the others with you?' The frightened man stuttered, wide eyed. 'I did nothing, I don't know.' Bobby Brooks had no intention of giving up. His voice bellowing. Eyes piercing into the face of the cowering figure before him.

In sheer terror of the giant standing over him, Paul Fowler spoke. 'I, I, found her. Laying on the ground, face down. I turned her over. Thought she was dead. They scared me. I saw them running off. They could have seen me come back. I ran, just ran.'

'Why didn't you phone the police?' Sobbing, his entire body rocking. 'No phone. I don't have a phone. I didn't want to be involved.' Years of experience told the Inspector the wreck in front on him was telling the truth.

'I believe you, now I need you to tell me everything you remember.' Paul Fowler swallowed huge gulps of tea. Grateful, he tried to calm down. 'She was in a pool of blood. I thought she was dead. No movement from her. I saw only their backs. They were running up the alley. It was dark. I only stopped for a piss.'

'Why didn't you come forward?' Bobby Brooks knew the answer already. 'I saw nothing.' He pleaded. 'I'm too weak, I have nothing. Couldn't have fought them off. I thought it was a man lying there.' He rubbed a greasy forehead. The liver damage his years of drinking had caused showed in the yellow of his eyes.

Once an engineer who earned thousands on the rigs. Now his senses swam in a river of toxic waste. His memory shot. He tried to remember. The concentration too much, he bent over, collapsing to the floor. Further questioning pointless.

Bobby left him to pull himself together. How much he could rely on his evidence was questionable. Twenty minutes later they restarted the interview.

'I saw long red hair, that's when I knew it was a woman. I looked up. There were four of them at the top of the alley. One had blonde hair, I'm sure, a short leather coat as well. I remember hearing a Yorkshire accent. Didn't see the two in front, but the one at the back had a goatee. Am I in trouble?'

He went on. 'One had a Castleton Rovers scarf. I know, I used to have one. I know the colours. Black hair, one may have had black hair. Not sure, sorry. I'm sorry.'

It wasn't much. Vague descriptions, but more than they had. If he was right, they were local. He'd make sure he had officers posted at home matches. Check fans at the gates. He could get a breakthrough.

Booked for withholding information following a crime. Paul Fowler was free to go. Now he had to tell Eddie Boyle he was no further forward. That he didn't relish.

TORMENTED

Bobby got to work, back checking home match dates. There had been a match on that day. It could well have been a Rovers scarf seen at the crime spot. It was a breakthrough of sorts. A long time coming, but better than nothing.

The Rovers ground, a short distance from Baker Street and the Half Moon. He was sure that is where they would have been drinking. It was the pub of choice for a post-match booze up. This is where he would start.

It would be a long-drawn-out process. He knew that, but with extra officers surging throughout the Town chasing serial killers. He could spare an officer. It was three years past. The descriptions, accurate or not, would have changed.

The decision made to visit Eddie. Tell him the information direct. Eddie deserved that.

Bobby arrived at the apartment, pressed the bell, heard Angel's voice ask him in. The door was ajar when he reached the apartment. Angel and Eddie waiting for news.

In true detective mode, the description of the mystery woman came to his mind as he greeted Angel. He shrugged off his thoughts. It was unlikely that Angel Boyle would dress and act like a tart, Let alone slum it down the Moon. The woman had green eyes; they were emphasised by witnesses. Angel had blue. He smiled.

A tired Eddie stood by his daughter. He looked ill. Pallid, unwell. 'He's been ill.' Angel read his thoughts. 'His liver isn't functioning as it should. They're doing tests.'

Heavy drinking may have been in the past for Eddie. The aftermath was not. He had felt unwell for some time. Nausea, tiredness, dizzy. Ignored it as he would. Now he had to face it. Constant bouts of diarrhoea followed by periods of constipation had forced him into action.

A thorough examination, blood tests and CT scan were done. The results he hadn't expected. He had kept them from Angel. Medication would sort it out.

Dr Morton, a sallow-faced man, had treated Eddie for years. Knew his personal history. The best of a bad bunch to Eddie. He hated doctors. Seen enough with Carrie. Dozens of pills, talking to psychiatrists who failed to help her. Confused the shit out of her. He loathed them with a passion but remained sensible enough to know when something was wrong. Then, only then, did he seek help.

An urgent call from the surgery had Eddie worried. A smiling receptionist greeted him, informed him Dr Morton would be with him shortly. Reluctantly, he sat down. Eyed up the creaking gates, forever at the surgery. Demanding attention, putting the NHS in jeopardy. He hated the clinical atmosphere, giving false hope to patients as millions of germs found new victims.

Thankful when the tannoy sprang into life. 'Mr Boyle to Dr Morton's office.'

Unnerved at the normally rude doctors' kindness. Eddie wanted answers. 'Well, tell me it straight.' 'I always tell it straight Mr Boyle. You have alcohol related liver damage, causing hepatitis. Provided you stay off the booze, the liver will heal itself.' Eddie picked up on the graveness etched on the doctor's face. He wasn't convinced.

'If not?' questioning Dr Morton, Eddie's yellow tinged eyes focussed on his face. The doctor shrugged his shoulders. 'Up to you. There will be further tests, sooner rather than later.' He nodded in agreement.

Back at the apartment well before Angel arrived. Eddie had his story planned, ready for the questioning he would get from his daughter. She was now relaying the same story to Bobby. Protecting him, it's pleased Eddie. He knew he could rely on her as he always had before.

Glad of the coffee, Bobby perched himself on the edge of a chair. 'I have news for you both about Carrie's assault.' In an instance, all thoughts of illness had gone. Now intense eyes watched the detective.

As she nestled by her father, Bobby began. 'I interviewed a suspect at length. It turned out he had no part in the assault. He could provide some information.' He knew he had to be careful. Much as he wanted to tell his old friend all he knew. He couldn't. He had protocols to follow.

Eddie, aware he would never get a name out of his buddy. Listened. Angel, more forceful, pushed hard for information. 'There were four men, the witness thinks. One had a Castleton Rovers scarf. That's all I have for you but I'm on it, that I promise you.'

Angel grimaced. Four of them. The pain her mother must have felt. The sheer fear. She felt sick to the stomach. Four, her imagination again at the scene. Her mother on the floor, being kicked, beaten, raped. Laughing at her, taunting her. No mercy shown to her. The number ran around her mind. She had work to do and wouldn't stop until caught, or work was completed.

Angel led Bobby to the door. He wished Eddie a speedy recovery, turned, repeated. 'I won't let this go; I will get these bastards.' With that he left, leaving father and daughter contemplating the information.

It all fit. The match had been a championship, so changed to a Sunday night. A match was playing. They wouldn't be regulars. Eddie was sure of that. They all knew Carrie; none would have attacked her. It had to be football scum. A lot had been in the Moon that night.

'They had to be local Angel. Only locals would still be there.'

'I pray every night that they are caught. It could become a reality.' Angel had stopped listening; she was visualising her presence at the next after match booze up. The hug she gave her father as she left, making him promise to eat, filled him with hope.

An extra-long workout allowed her to vent her anger. Release her body from unwanted feelings arising out of the fresh evidence.

Suspicions Aroused

He didn't feel well; he felt very unwell. Angel hadn't called. The tablets weren't easing the pain he was feeling. He needed support. A walk in the fresh air would help, but the effort needed to put his coat on too much.

Further tests had been arranged, leaving Eddie with a foreboding. Tricks played by his mind went over and over the growing mountain of information about the killings. Detectives were still milling all over the Town. The mystery woman had never come forward, nor seen by anyone.

Not drinking, he hadn't been to the Moon for a while. Now he wanted to. See who came in. Be back on his feet, moving again. Illness was something he detested, especially his own. It was that feeling down that brought Carrie's torment back to him. He'd seen enough of sickness to last him a lifetime.

TORMENTED

The combination of drugs he was taking didn't agree with Eddie. Being told what to do disagreed with him more. Few comforts were left for him now. The odd drink was one of them. Told not to drink at all angered him. He had been suffering mood swings. Nauseous much of the time he was getting depressed.

He focussed more these days on Carrie than he had done in a while. Birthdays, anniversaries, special occasions. Memories of quality times. All were more frequent nowadays. His mood, happy or sad, dependent on the recall. Back in his own bedroom had a therapeutic effect. Here he found peace, quietness. Ask for forgiveness, thought he heard her voice.

Eddie placed great effort in keeping the room clean, as Carrie left it. Her clothes remained in the wardrobe. Cosmetics still on the dressing table. Everything as it was. To move them a step too far for him. A job for another time. That time wasn't now.

Determined to pull himself out of his current mood, he kissed the photograph of Carrie, sitting on the sideboard. Opened the long draw, took out his notepads, news articles and a bulging A4 file. Focussing on his work would take his mind from his sickness.

As he reviewed the jigsaw pieces, one by one, he became submersed in his task. It took several minutes for him to realise the shrill sound of the ringing phone breaking through his silence. A worried Angel on the other end.

Her tone was sharp, Angel hated waiting for anything. She also hated phones, using them only when there was an actual need. Today was an actual need. She was enquiring about her father's health.

With an apology, he explained what he was doing. His daughter's tone changed. Lying, she told Eddie she had bought him some fruit and was bringing it. An excuse to glean anything new he might have found.

It was an ideal opportunity. Eddie was meticulous in his notes. The minutest detail written down. A fact was a fact to her father. She would help him read all the facts without casting suspicion on herself. Together they would sift through the information for missed clues. The prospect excited Angel.

A large mound of notes lay spread across the table, floor and chair. Each dated. Interviewees name, address and relationship to the case. Shared across A5 sheets, filed under headings.

A special ability to keep various pieces of odd information shared by Eddie and Angel. Each could decipher strange things, put them together like a jigsaw puzzle. Something Bobby Brooks had recognised in Eddie years ago. His skill used to unravel many cases.

TORMENTED

On route, Angel picked up some fruit. Gave it to her father. 'Where shall we start?' 'The nationals, who knows.' Eddie was far from complimentary. 'Begin cross referencing. Correct details only with my articles. The common points need noting.' It was the last thing Angel wanted. It was the file marked 'Mystery Woman' she preferred.

Page after page thumbed. Angel, bored, continued to compare the reams of information. Salient notes made as she did so. Each fact placed under its correct heading. The nonsense statements made by overzealous journalists ignored.

At last she turned to the file marked 'Mystery Woman'. Her interest renewed. All agreed on the short red dress, high heels and green eyes. At that point it stopped. Some said red hair, others brown, brunette, blonde. The description given of the coat varied from white to cream. Short to long. They gave height from 5'7" to 6'0". In a court of law, none would hold up.

'The descriptions of the mystery woman, the one who left the pub before the victim. So poor, it could be a thousand distinct people.'

Eddie stopped. He said nothing. It was unusual for his daughter to get a fact wrong. He was being silly. Mental reassurances failed to put his mind at rest. 'Left the pub before the victim?' Angel knew her father will. She tensed. His next question putting her on alert.

'The mystery woman's clothes, they sound like those your mother was wearing when attacked.'

On the defence, she snapped. 'How would I fucking know? You didn't bother to tell me, remember?'

'I never told Bob either. Just strange.'

Had she slipped up. Did he know, suspect? His eyes fixed on hers.

'32, why dig a knife into someone's chest to carve a number? What could that be? It must be significant, but what?'

He scratched his head, look puzzled. Angel knew him better.

'What the fuck are you asking me for? Ask Inspector Brooks. The fucking detective, you know, your pal. Murder, I think it means fucking murder, okay. The fucking clothes a coincidence. That's what I think?'

Indignant, she stared hard at her father. He had a choice. Push his irrational theory, lose his daughter. Move on, strengthen the bond. He chose the latter.

Now angry, holding her emotions in check, Angel spat 'Any dafter, fucking questions or shall we carry on?'

TORMENTED

Eager to continue, Eddie went back to his notes. Angel read the interviews with the victim's partners. She spoke, her voice cold. 'It fascinates me. They were so fucking perfect. Heroes. worshipped by their families. Loving, kind, blah pissing blah.'

Half to herself, part audibly, she added. 'So why then were they out all hours. Pissed, looking for an easy lay?'

'Come on Angel, not all men are dangerous for enjoying a pint or fancying a lass.'

Angel rounded on her shocked father.

'It was four such scum that raped, battered and murdered your fucking wife.'

Angel had changed, he knew that. Her mother's death, having more impact on her than he realised. How much alarmed him.

'They deserve what they get.' The words stressed, challenging Eddie to respond. He didn't. It occurred to him that counselling may help. He mentioned it.

A look of icy contempt shot from her. 'Did it help your wife; shall I just hang myself now?' Eddie was silent. Sick to the pit of his stomach.

The next six hours passed, part in silence. Part in awkward conversation. Piece by piece, information sifted, documented. Highlighted, filed. To break the deadlock, Eddie suggested a break for food. Angel, eager to discuss the findings, agreed.

Marker in hand, Eddie flip charted ideas. The authentic story. He hated journalists who half interviewed, made up headlines. Sullied the repute of the profession. Poor attitudes, bad writing, unpleasant manners.

Now calm, Angel took the pen. 'You look tired, let me write.' Eddie smiled. Nodded. More relieved than tired. With an illness he could cope. Conflict with his daughter, scared him. The heading on the chart read:

KEY POINTS

Point 1	**Three male victims in 5 months**
Point 2	**No found relationship between victims**
Point 3	**MO same – stabbed, partly clothed, 32 Carved in chest.**
Point 4	**2 victims (1 wound) 1 victim (2 wounds)**
Point 5	**No evidence of sexual activity**
Point 6	**No evidence of robbery**
Point 7	**No similarity in ages**
Point 8	**High alcohol content found in bodies**
Point 9	**No apparent motive**

Lack of real forensic evidence annoyed Eddie. Too many outsiders slowing up the procedures. Interfering with evidence. CIA reporters, sight seers. No additional information in weeks. No nearer to finding a killer. The strangeness of a man killing men for no apparent reason. None of it made sense.

'Something's missing. We've overlooked something. I'm determined to find out what.

Angel listened to her father. His words made her uncomfortable. If anyone could make the link, it would be him.

Eddie now looked tired. It had been an endless day. A memorable day spent working with his daughter. He enjoyed that even with the awkward moments. Angel, likewise, but with different motives. Now, she realised she was safe from discovery.

Angel did not want her father to delve deeper into their conclusions, so advised him it was time for her to leave. Rest take his medication and forget it for tonight. Smiling. Relieved they were okay again, he nodded. Hugged his daughter and saw her to the door.

Body aching, restless. Eddie's mind spinning. Rest was eluding him, and it annoyed him. So many questions without answers. Why was his daughter so angry, challenging? Why was she so interested in the murders? He tried hard to dismiss the thoughts from his head but could not. The description of the mystery woman. No sexual motive. Why a man would kill other men for no reason? So many facts made little sense.

Every instinct he had told him he knew the answer. He refused to give them credence. He had to be wrong, it couldn't be. His senses were being pushed and pulled around. The more he fought his own reasoning, the more the bricks fell into place.

Angel was powerful. With contact lenses, fit the description. Never bothered with boyfriends. Detested drunks. Piece by piece, the jigsaw was falling into place. Was the killer a man OR a woman? How much had Carrie's death affected on his daughter? He reeled, his World about to crash about him. There was no other rational solution.

The questioning, the need for minute detail. Eddie felt sick. He saw it so clearly now. She had pushed Bob for every fact. He sat bolt upright. 'Why didn't I see it?' Aware of his daughter's split personality. Her ability to move from caring to cold in an instance, he knew only too well, she could be capable of stabbing someone if she was in danger.

God.......... at that moment he wanted to join Carrie more than ever before. He held his head. The thoughts hurt him. His heart pumped fast. He felt his chest was fit to burst. He had to make decisions but didn't know if he could make them.

TORMENTED

Richard Travis

There was no time to waste. Angel was aware of how good her father was at his job. Time was running out for her, and her work was still incomplete.

Tired, the day with her father had been challenging and long. It wouldn't be long before he made the links. No time to sleep, she needed to get ready.

Different clothing was now needed. Her mother would understand. She grabbed her bag, popped brown contacts in. Changed and left the building. The night was crisp, nippy. Her watch read 10pm. To get near the Moon in time, she would need to hurry. Once it turned 11pm, her chance was gone. Too many people in the streets. Potential witnesses she could do without.

Reckless, she hailed a taxi. 'Drop me off at the top of Baker Street.' The driver nodded and revved his engine. Angel kept her head down. She had deepened the colour of her lipstick, her hair remained in bunches. Tied back, the wig she wore was now blonde. The younger she looked, the more men she would attract.

The bastards she came across at night always liked young girls. She hated their hypocrisy. Stalwartly citizens by day. Preying cobras by night. Enraged by the praise heaped on them, false news. They were neither loyal nor good men. They were no different to the piranhas who had attacked her mother. Destroyed her family. Angel felt nothing but contempt. No compassion, no remorse. None was shown to her mother, and none would be shown to her victims.

Drunks, parasites, scum of the earth. They made her bilious. A shiver ran through her spine. Her stomach was heavy. Tonight's kill could be her last. She wasn't as prepared or alert as she liked to be. It didn't matter. She must carry out her plans. Avenge her mother.

A mist descended, leaving a halo glowing around the illuminated lamp post. It was quiet, almost serene. Momentarily, she wanted to be back in the taxi on her way home. She felt dejected. Alone, empty. In a race against her own father's intuition.

Distracted by a door opening on the street, she watched. A man stepped out behind him, a woman.

TORMENTED

They embraced, she stepped back in. He turned and headed toward Angel. No doubt on his way back home to his wife, the lover satisfied. A piece of shit, nothing else.

He looked fit, smart, late-forties, she estimated. Black hair, ruffled. She thought. He was shagging someone else's wife behind his innocent partner's back. Maddened fury built up inside of her.

As he got level with her, she gave him a wide smile. He smiled back, walked past her. Annoyed, she dropped her bag. There was no time to mess. Stooping down, she stumbled forward. He turned back. 'Need help there?' He smiled at her again. Thanking him for stopping, she smiled back. An inviting smile. Brown eyes, wide and tempting.

Richard Travis took it as an invitation. Angel Boyle meant it as one. 'Walk you home, it's late to be alone in the street.' He looked her up and down, puzzlement etched on his face. It didn't go unnoticed. They walked together, passing several alleyways. She waited for his move. There was none.

No dirty talk, no improper suggestions. No attempt to touch her. His only conversation an explanation of the dangers of being out alone at night, dressed provocatively. Taking umbrage at his comments, she spun on him. 'Why are you telling me this stuff? I suppose I'm a slag because I dress nice. Am I? Her question was direct and acidic.

'Sorry?' he looked perplexed. 'I know you, don't I? He looked hard at her. Angel was unnerved. 'Carrie Boyle. You're her daughter, aren't you? You look like her. I know you from school. I'm a teacher. Your mother used to drop you at the gates. I remember. A good-looking woman.'

In shock, Angel tried to think fast. He knew her mother. Was he one of her attackers? It fell into place. She wanted it to fall into place. As they reached the next alleyway. 'Up here.' Her voice was quiet. He walked behind her, noticing her shapely legs. The cobbled narrow street was dark, gates hung off their hinges. Net curtains covered the windows, tatty, in need of washing.

Debris littered the ground, typical of alleyways in Baker Street. Whilst fronts of houses may have been looked after, the backs were common ground. Neglected and dirty.

They were halfway up now. Still, he tried nothing. Did he drag her mother up a similar alley? Was her mother more desirable than her? Did pack mentality play a part? 'Do you think my mother dressed inappropriately if you think I look like her then?' Richard Travis stopped in his tracks. Surprised at the coldness in her manner.

'I wish I'd never stopped to help you now. I'm trying to help. Keep you safe because I remember you and yes, I remember your mother. A gracious woman. That's it.'

Angel spun on him, wild, furious, slapping his face hard. 'You mean it's your fucking guilt.' She spat. He was strong, twisting her arm. She whimpered in pain. 'You need a fucking psychiatrist; I have no idea what you're fucking saying.' She raised her other arm, caught him with a clenched fist. Now angry, he held both of her arms as she flayed wildly. 'Is this what you did to my mother, Bastard?' Her voice, now a growl.

He, as most of Castleton, knew of Carrie Boyle's demise. Compassion filled him. It was obvious that the effect on her daughter was greater than anyone thought. She needed medical help. He realised that. He wasn't the person to tell her, he knew that as well. Releasing her arms, he spoke reassuringly to her.

'I'm a married man. I did nothing to your mother and I'm doing nothing to you but trying to get you home safe. Think.'...... His words trailed off as the knife pierced his heart. It was quick. His body went limp, his eyes staring. A shocked look on his face.

She shook as she worked. The knife twisted deep into his flesh, the number 32, red and raw, carved into his forehead. Finished, she smiled as she watched the blood run the length of the gully, thick and fresh. She wanted to hurt this one. She spat at the blank eyes.

Unzipped her bag, took its contents out one by one. Minutes later, she had changed into a tracksuit and trainers. Pulled on the brow wig, stuffed her bloodied clothing into a black bin bag.

She broke into a sprint, bumping into a couple as she exited the Baker Street. Not stopping to apologise she continued to run, followed by a tyrant of abuse from the man.

Panic filled her. What if they could recognise her? Had they found the body? She slapped herself hard. 'Stop it. They can't recognise you. Calm yourself NOW.' Heart beating fast, she entered the door, locking it at once behind her.

Relaxed, safe, she piled the blood-soaked clothing into the washer. Threw in a tablet, slammed the door shut. The whir of the motor had a calming effect on her. Sighing, she reached for the polishing cloth, wiped her shoes clean and headed for the bathroom.

Hot water ran over her skin. The aroma of oils and scented candles rose with the stream of steam rising towards the ceiling. She sank below the foam, submerging herself. It felt good, blocked out her thoughts.

Re-emerging, panic gone, she thought of her mother. 'I got one of them tonight, I know I did. Are you pleased with me? It was close, though; I must be more careful.

Might have to stop for a while. You won't mind. I'm getting tired. Making mistakes, mum.' In her heart she knew this had been a suitable target. Why else make the comments? He wanted her to know. He needed to be punished for his sins. She had given him his wish.

Police sirens broke into her peace, interrupted her thoughts. The carcass had been found. It was quick. CID and local force officers would flood the area. The news would reach her father. Illness would not stop him going to the site. She'd contact him in the morning. Now, it was time to retire, resume her talk with her mother. Follow her routine after she had been at work. It was an important cleansing process.

Angel lay back on the soft sheets. Pulled the Murano blanket around her neck, took a swig of the brandy by her bed, popped a tablet and closed her eyes. 'Sometimes I wish I were with you Mum. I miss you. You're looking after me, I know that, but I get lonely. He's not well. I know he's not. I'm trying to forgive him. He caused this. It's hard.'

It didn't take long for Carrie's presence to enter the room. She smiled at Angel, the same beaming smile she always shared with her daughter. An aura shone around her, filling Angel with happiness. She knew her mother was pleased.

Engrossed in a game of computer chess when her mobile rang. Angel had slept well, felt fresh, alert. Her morning jog done; breakfast finished. All was well. Breakfast was her major meal of the day. Important for energy. She never missed it. Ever careful of eating stodge, it comprised one slice of toasted granary bread, a poached egg, black coffee and one rasher of bacon. The fat removed.

Breakfast was as much a routine as most thing in her life. She had sat to eat, as always, at her set table. Not letting anything disturb her, she waited before turning on the TV.

Castleton killer strikes again! It was all over the news. It showed Baker Street, teaming with reporters, police and freaks who enjoyed the macabre. A reporter interviewed Bobby Brooks live from the scene. Bobby was saying nothing other than to repeat they welcomed the help of profiling experts now working alongside them.

He added that the net was closing in on the killer. Bravado, Angel murmured. She knew they didn't understand who they were seeking. Her father's notes had helped to keep her up to date with findings.

She scanned the faces in the crowds. Her father was nowhere. Part of her wanted to go there but it a risk too far. She had to wait. Too keen wasn't too clever.

She turned on her computer to a chess challenge awaiting her. A stranger from across the pond, she played. She gained a sense of achievement beating faceless strangers. People she wouldn't ever meet, nor want to meet. She enjoyed the game, forcing an En prise before capturing their key pieces. Ruthless in her approach to the game, no opportunity for escape given.

Annoyed, she grabbed up the phone. Her father's voice sounded unfamiliar. Distanced, anxious. Had she made a mistake? Left a clue in her anger? A knot tightened in her stomach. Was she becoming sloppy? Did it even matter? There was little normal life left for her now. She knew that.

'Have you heard the news, Angel?' Desperation rang in his voice. They have found forensics. Her mind reeled. Forensic evidence, impossible, she reasoned. 'I'm going to the station, talk to Bobby. There's a press release at 11am. I need to see you then. Be here at 2pm. His words were stressed. This was an order not an ask. His tone told her no excuses. She had to be there.

The television cracked into life. Angel waited for the press release. It wasn't Bobby Brooks but a CID officer who made the statement. Inspector Brooks had been pushed to the side lines, the case now being too big.

'I'm Chief Inspector Gary Bentley.' He began. Angel stared at him. He cut an imposing figure. Tall, slim and with an air of authority. He was, without doubt, an experienced officer. He waited several minutes for quiet, then spoke.

'Camera bulbs flashed in rapid succession. Microphones lined up to catch every word. 'Another murder was committed in Castleton yesterday evening. We believe the killings are being carried out by the same person. The victim, like the other victims, was stabbed. We are asking for anyone who saw anything unusual, however small, to come forward. We will catch this killer but need any help, you, the public, can give.'

A barrage of questions ensued from the press. Steely eyed, with a wave of his hand, he showed he had finished talking. Turned and walked back into the station. Stoney faced.

Filled with foreboding as she entered her father's apartment. She hoped that there was fresh news about her mother's killers. Deep down she knew that wasn't the case.

'Sit.' Her father's voice was cold, his expression icy. She obeyed without question. He looked at her in the eyes. 'DNA was found under the fingernails of Tom Davidson. It's the same as spittle found on this victim. A full DNA profile has been done. If it's a match on their database, the killer's reign is over.'

Angel's mind was a whirl. She had slipped up. She recalled spitting. Her hand reached up to where the scratch had been. Genuine panic was striking hard, churning up her guts. She felt herself shake. Aware that her father was watching her every reaction, she tried to calm herself.

She wanted to reach out to her father, for him to hug her. He didn't. There was always a chance of being caught, but not yet. It was too soon. She wanted to tell her father, unload the burden she carried. Make him understand. She couldn't. He had changed. Taken back his life. Coming clean could crush him. It wasn't a choice.

'Any further news about mother?' Angel was desperate to deflect the conversation. Eddie's eyes softened; tears welled up. Ignoring his daughter's question, he continued to narrate his conversation with Bobby Brooks to her.

The more he spoke, the more her heart sank. 'They're doing toxicology tests of the last victim. They know alcohol played a part in the first three, but not in this one. The guy was tee-total. It shocked angel. She knew the men who had raped her mother had been drinking in the Moon beforehand.

Sure, that Richard Travis had been one of the assailants. She now questioned her own beliefs. 'I couldn't have been wrong. All the signs were there. No, they've got it wrong. I know they have. What if I made a mistake? I don't make mistakes.' Her mind now played good cop, bad cop with her. She didn't like it. The thought of such a mistake assaulted her senses.

Not knowing what to do or say, she looked towards her father for guidance. The knowing look on his face brought tears to her eyes. A rarity for her. Affected by the display of genuine emotion. The vulnerability of his only child. Eddie deeply needed to protect her. He had to protect her.

His arms reached out, welcomed by Angel. For several minutes they stood locked together. He clasped her. They wept together.

It pained him to think of her as a killer. He knew that she had never been in trouble with the police, so the likelihood of her DNA being on file was remote. He needed to make this right.

Aware that the meeting he had had with Bobbie Brooks had meant a lot more than it suggested. Bobby was trying to warn him. Letting him know that they were closing in fast. Saying less than he knew but showing it in his eyes, his manner, his silences. How much they knew, he couldn't imagine. He reasoned if he was putting the picture together then trained officers were doing the same.

The tears in his daughter's large green eyes filled him with dread. He could feel her fear. Losing Carrie had been a burden that had proved almost too much to bear. He couldn't lose Angel. The only meaningful thing he had left in his life. Head pounding, he needed to think, needed to put things into perspective.

TORMENTED

He wasn't a well man, the medication he was taking wasn't doing the job anymore. He should rest, take life easy. Instead he wanted the ground to open, swallow him. End his pain. Take away the numbness of his mind. This wasn't the life he intended for himself. There should be a loving wife by his side. He should have a daughter, settled and happy, grandchildren by now. Doing a lot of things but it wasn't to be. Life had dealt him some grave blows; this he didn't understand.

As he stood staring at the daughter he no longer knew or understood, he felt lost. Not knowing what to do, what to say. This was an unknown experience; one he didn't like. He didn't know what to do. Lost in his daughter's agony. He had to think, plan, put things right. Above all, he had to keep his daughter by his side.

Angel was his life now, his everything. His mind was racing. Dare he ask her outright? Challenge her with the most horrendous reality there could be. Confused, in a daze, words poured out. Irrational, non sensical in the situation.

'Angel, what about another book tour? Its time? I could come with you.' His words trailed off. What the hell was he saying, thinking. Time, that's all he wanted, time.

Now settling down, the initial fear that had overwhelmed her, subsiding. It would be good to keep a low profile for a bit. They couldn't link any DNA to her, of that she was sure. Her father was panicking for nothing, he knew nothing. Suspicions didn't mean guilt. They had no reason to suspect a woman. Her senses were working flat out.

Get away, it was a plan. An escape route, thinking time. The men she had killed deserved it; of that she was sure. All doubts of their innocence left her as quickly as they had arrived. Angered by her outburst, she felt incensed. Now she needed to regain composure, take back control.

In an instance, all show of weakness gone. Vulnerability diminished into invisibility. Angel was now cold and controlling again. 'I'll make us some coffee, you sit down.' It was an instruction, not a request. Weary, his body aching and tired, Eddie dropped into the easy chair.

A decision to keep his thoughts to himself was a wise one. He knew he would gain nothing by challenging Angel. Also, the effort would be too much for him to bear. Quiet, peace, reflection, time is what he needed. His daughter had to have help, that being the only certain thing at this point.

He needed a professional, the kind he was not. A plan, time to think. Above all, he needed to sleep. He needed Carrie; she always knew what to do. Exhausted, he fell into a tormented sleep. The kiss on his forehead, special, meaningful, not felt.

TORMENTED

Police forces from across the region were now trawling Castleton. Eddie failed to understand how any killer had murdered again and again under their noses. It didn't make sense. He had watched officers, two abreast, walking the length of Baker Street. Did they have any clue who they were looking for? He hoped not.

Sleep had done nothing to allay his fears. Unproven fears, he reasoned. He had to stop thinking this way. Continue and his daughter was lost to him for good, that he knew.

'Feel better dad?' Puzzled, Eddie took the coffee being held out to him. It was warm. 'You know, I'm due a meeting with my publisher. So.... I thought, yes, dad's right. A few days in London would do us both good.'

Not knowing how to respond, Eddie finished the drink. Angel smiled, stood up. 'Enough for today, dad. I'll book the reservations. It will help both of us.' With that, she was gone.

PATRICIA A SUTCLIFFE

The Results

The clinical odour in the waiting room stung Eddie's senses. He hated such places. Surgeries were for ill people, not for him. Eddie hated waiting anywhere. He scanned the room, allowing his reporter's head to take over. One by one, he eyed each patient, working out their stories. It was a game he often played. It gave him amusement. His ability to read body language was second to none. Combined with years of training, a sound intuition and logical mind enhanced his game.

A white-haired, frail old man faced him. He was clutching his wife's equally frail hand. About 80ish, Eddie surmised. The wife of the patient. Of that he was sure. The dullness in her eyes showed that she was ill. He smiled as she struggled to stand in answer to her name being called.

'Eddie Boyle.' The tannoy cracked into life. Dr Morton was sitting in an imposing green studded leather chair.

TORMENTED

His sizeable frame filling the generous seat area. Ben Morton was a balding man, plain speaking and brutal to those who wasted his time.

In a deep, resounding voice he addressed Eddie. 'I have the results Eddie, it's not good news.' He rubbed his eyes, as if struggling with his next words. 'It's liver cancer Eddie.'

Half listening, he tried to focus on the lengthy explanation Ben Morton was mechanically talking him through. 'Any liver cancer is difficult to cure. Primary liver cancer is hard to diagnose early, when it's still at a stage where it can be treated.

Secondary or metastatic liver cancer is hard to treat, it has already spread by then you see.' Eddie didn't see. He didn't see at all. 'Most treatment we give concentrates on making you feel better rather than being a curative measure.'

'If the tumour is at an early stage, we can remove it, but I have to warn you that many liver cancers are inoperable. The liver is already too damaged to save. Advanced liver cancer has no standard curative treatment, Eddie. Chemotherapy and low dose radiotherapy may help control its spread and ease your pain.'

'I can give you strong painkilling medication with other medicines to relieve your nausea and any swelling you get. It will also improve your appetite.'

Eddie was numb. This was serious, too serious to take in. 'Cancer of the liver!' He repeated the words several times. The nausea, the headaches and weight loss. Now he understood why he had felt so ill over the past several weeks. There had been no swelling but an overwhelming feeling of lethargy.

'Ironic Doc when Carrie passed all I wanted was to follow her. Be with her. Rid of this torment. Now, I'm getting what I want, but I don't want it.'

The information he had received had been stark and honest. Trying to get his head around it Eddie asked a direct question. 'How long Doc?' Ben Morton looked at him before replying. 'I don't know is the truth. It could be years if you take the medication, have chemo and stop the drinking all together.'

Concern for Angel welled up inside of Eddie. Almost breaking down, he fought, fought hard to keep his dignity. She had lost her mother in the most gruesome way. Now she would lose her father. He needed to glean every detail he could to plan, prepare her.

'It depends upon the rate that the liver tries to repair itself which will be down to the extent of the damage to it. Ben Morton was trying to keep to the facts. Tell it as it was without the emotion. Aware of the drink problem his patient had battled with, he couldn't help but feel compassion.

'Talk me through the process, step-by-step Doc, I need to understand what will happen.'

Dr Morton explained that they would carry out further tests and a biopsy to determine the extent of the damage. Chemotherapy would then start to try to shrink the cancer, containing it to the liver. Eddie sighed. The last thing he wanted was more tests. Nor did he want to endure months of chemotherapy being prodded and poked.

Only Angel was stopping him from going home and drinking himself to death. A far easier way out of the torturous slow-motion escape that had been explained to him.

'And, if I don't have chemo but just take the medication. What then?'

Ben Morton widened his eyes at the question. His forehead forming deep ridges. He shook his head. 'Go home. Consider your decisions. I'll arrange the tests. If you want me to speak to your daughter.'

His voice raised; Eddie stopped the doctor in mid-sentence. 'NO, absolutely not.' Assertive and almost shouting. 'NO, no one is to know, and Angel is not to know. No one, doctor, no one.'

With that, the consultation was over. Eddie moved towards the door. He could have caught a taxi or bus to travel the two miles back to his apartment. His heart heavy and in a state of shock, he decided to walk. He needed thinking time. Put things into perspective. Understand what was happening to his body and to his daughter.

He would rip his liver out if he could. This was the worst time for this to happen. His life and mind were in perpetual turmoil. At the bottom of Baker Street, he glanced at his watch. The Half Moon would be open now. The heavy doors proved a struggle for the weakened man, but no barrier.
'A large brandy.'

In silence he sat, staring at the open fire, pondering his life. Its last remaining embers crackled and danced in the grate. The warmth washed over his face. He saw his life in the darkened coals. Where had it all gone? What had happened to the successful reporter who had everything? Beautiful, loyal wife. Renowned author for a daughter. Life was so good. Laughter and money in abundance. He had known and relished success.

A tear rolled down his cheek as he recognised the fragility of life. Eddie Boyle felt overwhelmed, the burden too heavy to carry. One night that should have been filled with celebration was all it had taken to destroy all he had worked for.

One conversation, one doctor. It gutted him. Had it not been for Angel he would have called time, ended it all. Now, she was a constant in his thoughts. What would he do about her? How could he support her? He gulped the brandy in one and headed for the door. Eddie had no intention of allowing anyone to see him in this state.

Up the street, he hurried. Past the ginnel that changed his life. Glancing into the grimy darkness as he always did, the misery of a single night bouncing back into his thoughts. It was a punishment he told himself he deserved.

If Angel were a murderess, what could he do? What would he do? The pieces fit together, but he was reluctant to admit it to himself. How could he challenge his daughter, share his theories with her? Suggest such a gruesome thing. His heart hung heavy with the uncertainty of the dilemma facing him.

The warmth Eddie found in his bed made it a sanctuary he welcomed. A part of him wished he hadn't been told the results. He would have gone to London, spent time with Angel away from it all. Unaware of the thing eating him from the inside. Not knowing anything about it, dying quickly.

At least Carrie would never know or see his suffering. A silver lining. He let a laugh escape into the room. He feared for his limited future. Not of death. That held no fear for him. His fear was for what he was leaving behind his daughter.

As a father, he hadn't been perfect. Long hours of work, at all times, day and night, had meant little spent with his child. He had accepted long ago that the closeness she had with her mother was expected. He knew he had a lot of making up to do. Now he was in despair, the cancer he saw as a ticking bomb. Time was running out.

It was hard to open up to Angel and now he wished he had made more effort. Hugged her. Told her everything would be all right. Watch her smile and thank him, call him dad again with warmth in her voice and love in her eyes. He had to make it right, but how? The question tormented him. Time on Earth was limited. He knew her freedom on Earth could also be limited.

The taste of brandy lingered in his throat. He stared at the papered, woodchip ceiling. Memories came flooding back. The emulsion he chose with Carrie. The laughter as paint dripped from his brush, landing on her head as she glossed the skirting boards. Nothing but distant dreams now, and even they were fading.

TORMENTED

The Dilemma

Sweat ran down Eddie's forehead. Visions of Carrie being attacked, raped, left for dead. Night tremors, horrors he couldn't escape. He found no peace in sleep, haunted by the shadows of men he couldn't identify. Monsters roaming Castleton, free.

Head pounding, he felt nauseous. He was being eaten alive, mind and body, and he knew it. Yet somehow, the forces of the night had brought with them some clarity. Now he understood why Angel could be a killer. Then, like a bolt of lightning, it struck him. He sat bolt upright. '32, fuck why am I so stupid. It makes sense.'

Revenge was a potent emotion. A strong driving force, Eddie understood this. Their lives left in turmoil whilst the rapists had walked free. Free to continue their debauchery. Ruining life after life.

The net was closing in, new forensic evidence. Bobby Brooks had told Eddie that a new profile of the killer was being released within the next few days. It could be today, he didn't know. What would they say, what had they found? He needed to get to Angel's, needed to speak to her.

As he stood looking up at the apartment, he realised he had never been here before. Angel had always insisted on coming to him. That was the past days, though. He was a boozer who would want a drunkard in their home. It was different now, they had become closer. Much closer.

Today she had no choice. He was outside and determined to go in. He had to speak to her. What he would say he did not understand. There was a lot to talk about, a lot to confess. He needed to be in a place she couldn't escape from. Couldn't make an excuse to leave.

The buzzer sounded. He felt fearful. It would surprise her, he knew that. Why could he say he was there? Why hadn't he phoned to tell her he would visit? Would he tell her about his illness? How could she cope with that? He hoped beyond hope, she wouldn't be angry.

He saw the blind twitch; knew she was looking at him. The door remained closed. Again, he pressed the bell, keeping his finger on the button. Stepped out into the road, making sure she knew it was him. The door clicked open. The building smelt of richness. A hint of pride came over him. Angel had done well.

Eddie walked down the deep pink, marble tiled hallway, towards the lift. Before the cancer he would have taken the stairs, now he was too tired to manage a few steps, let alone several flights. For a solitary moment he forgot his reason for being there. He was proud, smiling he entered the lift.

At the door to her apartment stood Angel. She looked uncomfortable, puzzled. Eddie pushed by her and entered the apartment. His eyes taking in the ambience. This was luxury, a luxury he had never known. 'You have your mother's taste for fine things Angel.' He was half smiling, half hoping he was welcome.

'Can I look around?' He saw the request shook that his daughter. 'Is that all right then?' His voice raised, light-hearted. He wanted to break the awkwardness. Their eyes met, Eddie recognised the unmistakable coldness in his daughter's eyes. It was a coldness he hadn't seen for a long time.

She waved her hand towards the bedroom. Eddie took the opportunity and began his tour. Dawdling, room to room, his eyes scouring every corner. It was perfect, everything neat in its place. Nothing appeared out of the normal. Dust didn't belong here, frightened away by the antiseptic odour he could detect in the air. She was more like Carrie than he had ever realised.

The bedroom furniture was expensive. He reached for the wardrobe handle only to feel his arm jerked back by Angel. Her strength startled him. He stepped away, shaken. 'Sorry, but that's personal space.' He detected a tremor in her voice. 'Why are you here dad?' Her eyes had softened.

He had noticed the fast change in his daughter's emotional state before. One minute nervous, the next scared, then hostile, cold, hard. He found her hard to read, hard to connect with, but he had no intention of giving up on Angel. He had let Carrie down. The same couldn't happen again.

He sat on the leather recliner, admiring the lounge. Refusing his daughter's offer of a drink, he wanted to get on with what he had come to say. Ignoring him, Angel walked to the kitchen area, took out a percolator and made fresh coffee. She needed to be alert. Aware from her father's face that his reason for evading his private space wasn't a pleasant one.

The coffee smelt good, strong. Eddie took a sip. The television cracked into life. Lights flashed; fluffy microphones filled the screen as reporters struggled to get close to Bobby Brooks. He spoke, his deep voice, authoritative and confident. Reading from a prepared script, his words cut through Angel like a pick hacking through ice.

His words were deliberate and slow. 'New forensic evidence taken from the last victim has led us to believe the perpetrator may not be a male.' A wave of shock resounded through the gathered crowd. Eddie looked at his daughter. She had turned pale, her eyes wide. She said nothing. Did nothing, just stood, fixated on the screen.

'Profilers describe this person as a psychopath. Someone, well built, strong. A keep fit fanatic with a deeply held grudge against men. More than likely someone, let down or abused by the men in her life. Extremely dangerous, meticulous in their approach. If not caught, we strongly believe that this person will continue their campaign. If anyone knows anything, anything at all, it is imperative they contact the police.'

As cameras clicked, the Inspector asked for questions. Hands shot up. Pointing at a face in the crowd, Bobby Brooks nodded. 'I'd just like to ask whether you are nearer to understanding the cuts on the bodies. What the numbers mean?' The answer was short.' No nearer. Next question.'

What evidence, Angel knew she had left nothing behind. There couldn't be any extra evidence. They were guessing, hoping for a breakthrough. As if reading her thoughts, Eddie broke into her silence. 'It's the saliva they are talking about Angel.' Anger welled up in her, why had she lost control, let her temper get the better of her. Again, her father's voice broke into her thoughts. 'Why Angel, why.'

His words shocked her. Stunned, she spun round, her eyes matching his glare. He repeated his words. This time Angel's green eyes softened; she bowed her head. 'Those bastards killed my mother, ruined our lives. Left you dead inside, left me.... They made me what I've become.'

A deep sense of longing filled Eddie's heart. Lost for words, he was numb.

'They deserved to suffer, deserved all they got, so why not?' She spoke with a conviction that scared Eddie. In an instance he recognised that his precious daughter no longer knew right from wrong.

'They weren't the men, Angel. Not the same men who attacked your mother.' Eddie tried to reason with his daughter, but to no avail. She glared at him. To her they were the same. Drunks who thought they could take anything they wanted from any woman they wanted it with.

Eddie tried again. 'They weren't the same men Angel.' This time her answer was more of a scream.' Fuck you, fuck them. They were nothing but slobs. Foul smelling bastards who got their excitement from raping innocent women. Grimy hands pawing at them. Talking filth.

Roughing them up. Taking pleasure from their pain. They fucking deserved it, every one of them. Fucking deserved it.'

The lack of any remorse non-existent. Eddie didn't know the person who now stood before him. He didn't want to know the person stood before him. The stress he was feeling, making him feel unwell. He needed to rest.

Her demeanour changing just as her anger had risen, so it waned, she became placid. Poured herself a fresh coffee as if the last ten minutes hadn't occurred. Who was this? Eddie was beyond despair. Why hadn't he seen how much it had affected her? Was he to blame, not being there for her? His mind swam in a fog of guilt and self-doubt.

She handed him a fresh mug of coffee. It was porcelain with a witty saying on the side. She smiled as he took it. It wasn't a genuine smile, more of a smirk which said. 'Yes, your daughter's a killer, now what?'

'Biscuit dad?' Eddie went cold. Stared at his daughter, now sitting relaxed, long legs crossed. Her face angelic. How, how could the girl before him commit such crimes? Take a knife and drive it through someone's body. Carve a tattoo onto their foreheads? How could she now act as if nothing had happened? Was she in total denial or did she just not care?

He crossed his mind that his daughter was unstable. Unaware of the reality of what she had done. The significance to others. The lives she had destroyed. It was too surreal. He felt himself wrenching. Took several deep breaths and laid his head back.

Part of him wanted to tell her he was dying. The obvious state of her mind stopped him. It would push her over the top. The final straw to send her into insanity. An insanity from which she may never return. He wouldn't be responsible for that.

'We have to talk about this Angel.' Her reply disturbed him. 'Talk about what?' Eddie explained. 'They will make the mystery woman the focus of their search now, Angel. Bob has already made joking comments about you looking like the description.'

Her answer abrupt, voice, controlled. 'They have no evidence linking anyone Father. They would have been an arrest if they had.' The word, Father stressed. Eddie was feeling weak, his head ached, and the sickness was rising in his stomach. The stranger in front of him remained calm, controlled. Matter of fact. A stranger who could kill in cold blood. His eyes drifted towards the telephone perched on the coffee table.

Eddie had never known his daughter or of her capabilities. Even as a child there had been a coldness about her. The only genuine warmth ever shown was to her mother, who doted on her. Angel had wanted for nothing, spending hours on end by Carrie's side, laughing, chatting. Being.

'What are we to do Angel?' She shrugged her shoulders. 'Join mother?' Recoiling at the flippancy of her answer, closer to his own thoughts than he cared to admit. He placed a hand on her shoulder. She twisted away and knocked it off.

'You need help, Angel. Actual help and I don't know how to help you.' Angel looked confused. 'I need help. Help for what? For avenging my mother's attack. Removing scum from the Earth. For caring enough for you both. Don't you understand I had to punish them for what they did. Ask mother, she will say the same.'

The detachment in his daughter's voice was something Eddie hadn't experienced before. She was talking about murdering four men as if it were a job. Something she did as a hobby, with no comprehension of the severity of her actions.

'You've caused pain to others. You've taken human life. Your mother wouldn't have wanted this, Angel.' His daughter smiled. 'Yes dad, she did. She told me. We had long chats about every one of them.' Her smile widened. Her eyes sparkled, she nodded.

Truth was painful, but Eddie had to face it. His daughter was a misandrist. He felt repulsion, love and fear at the same time. Each emotion fighting against the other for the top place. 'Did you know what you were doing?' Ignoring the question, Angel told him he looked tired and should rest.

Guilt-ridden thoughts filled him with angst. Was it his fault? Was he to blame for his absence during her childhood? Did she hate him as well? There had been times when he thought that. Surely, she couldn't really believe she talked to her dead mother. Carrie would never condone what Angel had done. He knew that. Sick to his stomach, head pounding, he slumped down, hitting the floor with a thud and into blackness.

A trickle of blood ran from Eddie's forehead where he had hit the edge of the coffee table. Angel, fearful for her father, scrambled to the floor where he lay. Seeing the blood, she rang 999.

The bright lights above the bed blinded him as he struggled to open his eyes. He tried to sit, the drip in his arm stopped him. Angel sat in a leather-backed chair; her eyes closed. She had been crying. Quietly, he called her name. Her eyes shot wide open. The cold, calculating woman he saw before he passed out, now gone. In her place, a loving, concerned daughter. Worry etched on her face.

She expressed a deep sense of relief as she relayed the events of his fall to him. 'Dehydration they said dad. You must drink more water. I'm pleased you are awake. I was so worried back there. You have stitches so don't move about.' His daughter was almost rambling out instructions. As she spoke, she leant over him and pressed a buzzer. Seconds later a nurse rushed into the room.

Within minutes he was being poked, prodded and a needle thrust into a canular in his arm. Eddie hated needles and grimaced at its sight. Cringing as the blood flowed into the tube. Deep and red. 'It's a good job your daughter was there, Mr Boyle. With a condition as serious as yours, it's important you pay attention to your water intake.

The white coated important looking man spoke before Eddie could stop him. 'You should be able to go home tomorrow if your tests are okay.' He smiled at them both. 'Now, it's rest for you. I've given you a sedative. It will make you drowsy.' With that, he turned and left the room. For once Eddie welcomed an injection. Angel's eyes told him he had a lot of explaining to do.

Now, however, he needed to rest. Not prepared or capable of giving answers. His head was pounding. He needed peace. He pretended to fall asleep, avoiding Angel's questions. Squeezing his shoulder, she tried to talk to him. Eddie lay still, made no movement but felt her hand squeeze his. It felt good. Slipping into a deep sleep to the sound of his daughter's footsteps on the tiled floor. Angel had given up and left the room. Tomorrow would be a new day. She would demand answers.

The sun was streaming through the window. It was one of those days that scream out, healthy walk. Eddie had woken early, his headache gone, replaced by a numb feeling across his forehead. His thoughts dwelling on the doctor's words and facing his daughter's inevitable questions.

He decided to tell her he had liver problems but nothing that couldn't be cured. A case of cutting out the drink. He would persuade her this had already ended. She would know nothing of his terminal cancer until she herself realised how ill he was.

Angel looked a vision entering the room. Red hair flowing, make-up immaculate, minimal but perfectly applied. Dressed in a green pencil skirt that brought out the beauty of her eyes. Navy blouse, green blazer and matching shoes. Eddie smiled, she was stunning, and it didn't go unnoticed by staff.

He admired her as she strode across the room. Tall and elegant. Admiration soon turned to sadness though as the image darkened. How could she carry out such atrocities? How could she think it was right to do so? He visualised her in a padded cell of some mental hospital. Lost, desperate, unaware of why she was there. It pained him.

The confusion in his own mind pained him more. One part of him told him to contact Bobby. To explain his daughter was disturbed. Plead with him to treat her leniently. Make sure she got the treatment she needed. The other side argued that he had to protect her. He wouldn't be on this earth long. He must make sure that was safe somewhere away from Castleton. That would mean him putting the police off the scent. How could he do that? He was dying. There had to be a way.

PATRICIA A SUTCLIFFE

On the Brink

Angel banged a chair down by the side of his bed. Startled back into the present, Eddie nodded to his daughter. 'You look beautiful.' It was clear she wasn't in the mood for compliments. She wanted answers. Piercing him with her eyes, she penetrated his gaze. It was the look that said she wasn't in the mood for any bullshit. 'Not here, Angel. When we get home.' His voice was soft but firm. She nodded agreement.

As they entered Eddie's apartment, Angel stooped to pick up mail from the doormat. 'Okay, I'm ready to talk to you.' Handing him the mail, she hesitated before seating herself on her mother's chair.

Eddie attempted to stick to the story he had planned in his head. His words, well-rehearsed, sounded plausible. 'I have a liver complaint, but I've stopped drinking and provided I don't slip back, it's treatable with medication.' The words flowed from his mouth. Angel was having none of it.

TORMENTED

'You won't mind if I talk to Dr Morton, then will you?' The bleeping of the answer machine came as a blessing to Eddie. He pressed the play button, listened to the message. It was Bobby Brooks, his voice urgent. 'Eddie get to me as soon as you get this.' He felt a sense of reprieve as he dialled the number. Angel's eyes clouded over in an icy mist. His indifference to what was so important apparent. 'Can't he leave you alone?' You're ill, you need to tell him.'

The news the inspector shared was grim. It had been concluded that the DNA taken from the scene could be that of a female. He explained that they had tested it for Y-chromosome genetic material, and none was present showing the possibility of a female. All women who frequented the Moon or lived in the area were being asked to take a DNA test. 'I was ringing to suggest Angel give a sample of her DNA just to rule her out from the investigation.

Without hesitation, Eddie informed him that his daughter was on a publishing tour. Angel looked at him, surprised. He looked back. His need to protect his daughter had taken over his senses. Angel saw red spinning on her father. 'I don't need you to lie for me. He can't force me to take any test. Anyway, it's not enough. They must prove you've been at the scene.

Angel showed no gratitude. She had done her homework. She knew that a DNA match was not enough evidence to charge her with murder. There could be many reasons DNA would be on a victim.

'Is it finished Angel?' 'Is what finished?' She teased her father. She knew full well what he was talking about. 'I'm serious.' He snapped. His patience wearing thin. 'It's finished, okay. Four for four.' For an instance, he despised his daughter. But he despised himself more. It tormented him knowing he should give his daughter in, frightened of the consequences to do so.

His life shortening by the day, he wrestled with his conscience. He couldn't turn the clock back, couldn't bring the victims back. Ease the suffering his daughter had, but he knew Angel was suffering just as much.

To leave this Earth knowing he had put his only kin in prison or, worse still, a mental home plagued him. He needed a friend to talk to. Carrie would have guided him, coached him to do the right thing. Carrie would have protected her daughter at all costs. It was decided. His daughter would not die in prison.

'Can we get to what really matters now dad?' Eddie wasn't going to squirm out of this one. He took his daughter's hand in his, led her to the settee. Not letting go of her hand, he began.

'I have liver cancer.' Both sat in silence for a while. Stunned, Angel stared ahead. Motionless in shock. 'It's not as bad as it seems. With medication I could be here a long time.' The bid of reassurance missed its mark totally.

She knew her father would try to hide the full truth from her.

'How long?' Her words seemed to echo in his head. A replica of his own words to Dr Morton. 'What have we done so terribly wrong that we have to suffer like this? Wasn't it enough to lose my mother?' Clasping her hand, Eddie bowed his head. 'I don't know, I just don't know. Things happen and sometimes we can't see a reason for them.'

He was voicing what she already knew. It wasn't helping. Aware that as a crime reporter, her father had followed some horrendous cases. People suffering for no obvious reason. In the wrong place at the wrong time. Was it fate? Bad luck. Some hidden universal justice.'

'Tell me everything you know about it, father. I need to know where we are at. What we can do. How much time I have with you?' At that, Angel broke down. What could he tell her? How much was there to tell her?

'My time is limited. No one knows how long, months, maybe years. I am getting weaker. I feel weaker some days more than others. I can have chemotherapy, but there's no guarantee it will help. I may live a bit longer, but it could also make my remaining time such poor quality it isn't worth it.'

It was more important now than ever before, to make sure that Angel was cared for. Made well again. His own illness was irrelevant to him. She had to be taken to a good place, but he was at a loss to know how.

Hesitantly, he put his arm around his daughter's shoulder. She accepted it. 'Angel, why would you think your mother is happy with what you've done?' One minute he was speaking to a concerned, loving daughter. The next, a cold-hearted murderer with no remorse or compassion for the misery she had caused.

Undeterred, he continued. 'Why would you possibly think that she would condone murder? To agree with your mutilating bodies, carving numbers into them. I love you, but you need special help. Let me get you through it. Please!'

Fury boiling up in her, Angel fought hard to keep her calm. 'My mother is the only person who ever loved me for me. She is the only person I ever loved. What right has some filthy drunk got to violate her body? Animals, nothing but feral monsters. By the way, FATHER.' The words were drawn out, her voice raised.

'They are LOWEST OF THE LOW. Have you got that? SCUM OF THE EARTH. My mother is overjoyed. She smiles with me when it's over. SMILES.'

TORMENTED

The very essence of her words crushed him. He wanted to reach out to her. Shake her back to reality. The staggering speed of the change in his daughter's emotions frightened him. The blood in his veins running cold. He tried to come to terms with the situation. Did she care whether he lived or died? Did she care whether she lived or died?

He studied her face. Was he capable of saving a daughter whose personality changed like the wind? Had she always been like this and he had missed the signs? As a child, hadn't she always been in control? In charge of everything she did? Never having the same friends for long. Preferred to be a loner. Was she always this person?

The furrows on Eddie Boyle's brow showed were deep, resembling troughs. Their presence highlighting the muddiness of his mind. He had struggled a long time to understand Angel. What made her tick, troubled by her lack of interest in boyfriends. Her preference to spend hours reading, writing. Activities that she enjoyed alone.

Was the happy childhood he thought his daughter had experienced all a sham? It had never occurred to him she was anything but happy. She had her moments. Is there a child that doesn't? It crossed his mind that maybe Angel had always had a mental illness, gone unnoticed. Was he too busy with his own life, his own ambition to see what was before him?

Was she to blame for the terrible things she had done? Did she even have a conscience? If not, he was more to blame for not caring enough to talk to her, listen to her. If she weren't in her right mind and had never been, could they hold her accountable?

Unable to convince himself, he had to look at the alternative. Was she in complete control? Knew what she was doing. Simply didn't care. He felt wounded so deep inside; it ripped at his very soul.

As if reading his mind, Angel articulated. Her tone soft and reflective. 'Dad, I seem to be in a mist. I'm going through the motions with no proper control. My mother speaks to me all the time. I hear her voice; Feel her pain. She shows me the agony she endured. I don't know who I am anymore, dad. I'm lost, dad.'

Her face, full of genuine emotion, disarmed Eddie. His pulses raced; his eyes stung. A terrible foreboding hung over him. The situation was hopeless, and he knew it. How long before he would succumb to the disease eating him slowly, painfully? If only he could close his eyes, click his fingers and end all of it.

Not waiting for a response. Angel continued. 'What did the doctor say to you? Have you sought a second opinion? What do I have to prepare myself for?' Each question direct and assertive. This was not someone who makes enquiries to gain answers. These were demands requiring solutions.

TORMENTED

He moved towards her, she moved away. Shook her head and instantaneously composed herself. 'Password.' She demanded, seating herself at Eddie's computer. Unquestioningly, he spelled out the password. The screen lit up. 'Liver Cancer.' The very words made him cringe.

An extensive list of articles came up. Scrolling down, stopping to read now and then. Angel made copious notes. Vulnerable, defeated. He did not understand what to do next. The emotion too great to bear, blindly observed his daughter's frantic scribbling. His mind elsewhere.

One by one, Angel went through all the treatment options. One by one, Eddie dismissed them. He wanted to die with dignity. Retain his senses until the end. There was a lot to arrange. A lot to resolve before he would allow the cancer to conquer him. Angel didn't agree but understood. Together they would put a plan in place. A plan they were both comfortable with.

The Suspect

No sooner had Angel fallen into a fitful sleep when she was woken by the piercing sound of her mobile. Sure, it was her father she chastised him. 'Dad, I've just managed to get to sleep. I'm tired, can't it wait?' A gruff voice, she registered as belonging to Bobby Brooks, responded. 'I need you to come to the station, Angel. I'll send a car, or I can come to you. Your choice.

The station was a familiar place. She'd sat here waiting for her father many times. As a child, Castleton Police Station had been like her second home. Briefings between her father and Bobby Brooks a natural part of Boyle family life. Now it felt a hostile place. The tone of the man she'd grown up admiring, matter of fact.

His face serious, professional, he stood before her. 'I've asked you to come here in an investigative capacity. Her red hair tied back, without make-up and looking pale. Angel didn't answer. The inspector noticed how her skin looked like porcelain. Her green eyes had lost their sparkle and now resembled frozen pools.

Officers were standing around outside the interview room. She had noticed their glances and felt unnerved. Many of the officers she knew by sight but had never felt the coldness she got from them now. They were whispering, pointing at her through the glass. Intimidated, she asked for the blinds to be drawn.

Bobby Brooks, broader than she remembered him, beckoned her to sit.

As a child she had once feared his powerful body, towering over her. Now, he was more her size, so why was she still fearful of him? Who was he? An aging police officer, an expert at his job, highly professional. Nevertheless, old and lined, the years of sleepless nights taking their toll.

For years, Bobby Brooks had been the face of law enforcement in the Town. Spending hour upon hour solving residents' problems as though they were his own. Keeping crime to a minimum. His reputation went before until now. Months of investigation, four unsolved murders, clues that led nowhere. He now looked dishevelled, broken. His ability to do the job questioned.

The Chief Inspector broke the silence. 'Do you know why I asked to see you specifically Angel?' Her head shook, indicating a negative. 'Look at the back wall.' Her eyes fixed on a Photofit of a young woman. Angel flinched but showed no emotion. 'Could be you. Same features, height.' He allowed his words to hang in mid-air. He watched carefully for a response. There was none.

'This woman was seen with one of the murder victims. We believe she could have something important to tell us. Something that may shed light on the killings.' They had nothing, and Angel knew it. A coolness in her answer. 'I don't understand why you think I can help you. So, it looks a bit like me, many people look similar. Are you trying to say you think it is me?'

Angel was now questioning Bobby, using his own techniques to fire back at him. Her composure never changing. Her voice matter of fact. He was getting annoyed and showed it.

Concrete evidence is what he needed before he could make any accusations. What he had was flimsy and would never hold up in a court of law. Ignoring the question and attempting to gain back his control, he continued.

'Can you remember where you were on June 19th and then again on December 2nd of last year?' Angel answered without hesitation. 'June I would have been on a book tour. December, I don't remember, but I wasn't in the Moon looking like a tart.' The sincerity of her answers made Bobby hesitate. Maybe he was barking up the wrong tree.

A resemblance to a Photofit didn't make her a killer. Then there were the distinct blue eyes. Hers were most definitely green. Was he grasping at straws, his own ego dented? Did he want to salvage it that much?

A tap on the door broke into his thoughts. In walked a sheepish newbie officer, two plastic cups shaking visibly in his hands. A pair of handcuffs hanging on his belt. Angel almost laughed out loud. He didn't look like he had the strength to carry the cups, let alone arrest someone.

As she sipped the watery drink, Bobby felt uneasy. He had wrestled over his friendship with her father. His reputation as an investigator. His humanity. Sat before him, an elegant youthful woman, a successful writer whom he had known since her birth. A girl he had comforted during the tragedies faced by the family. Spoke to when she needed the truth. Was she involved with such horrible crimes?

For an instance, he wanted to apologise to her. Tell her how sorry he was. How he had to investigate all angles. The seasoned police officer in Bobby Brooks was screaming at him. 'Get the DNA. The cup. Get it.'
'I'm just going through a process, Angel. The same way your father does when reporting on a crime.'

He was now standing behind her, hovering over her. She spun around to face him. She felt eyes peering at her through the cracks in the cream blinds. 'My father doesn't accuse me of being a suspect in a horrendous crime though. Does he?' With that she stood to leave the room. 'Here, I'll take your drink.' Angel smiled. 'I haven't finished yet; I'll take it with me.'

The door clicked as she turned the lock. Her father was still asleep in his bed. He looked pale, propped up on his pillow in an uncomfortable position. By his side, the remnants of a cold pot of tea.

His eyes opened and Angel saw the joy in them as he beckoned her over. He had so much to share with her. So many questions to ask her, but he was too ill. Their twisted conversation the evening before had left him crestfallen.

The redness in his eyes told her he had been crying. He would be told nothing about her summons to the station. Her conversation with his friend. It would serve no purpose. Instead, she apologised for causing him alarm. Told him she was going away for a few weeks. Book tours. See her agent, set up some readings. Do a few signings. It pleased him, as she knew it would.

The way he looked now; it was clear. He may not be here when she returned. Leaning over, Angel kissed him on the forehead. Her face warm on his clammy head. He blinked his eyes. He just wanted to sleep.

TORMENTED

Standing on the table, she noticed a bottle of tablets. Sorafenib 200mg read the label. Making a mental note of the name, she would look it up on the internet. Her father held his hand out, showing he wanted a tablet. Angel smiled, placed it in his palm, handed him a half-filled glass of water and watched him swallow it.

Dismayed at the pitiful sight on her father, she sensed it wouldn't be long until she was alone. Emotions mixed, she felt anger and sadness. How could she go anywhere with him in this state? He needed looking after; she was the only one he had.

'Stay in bed today dad. I'll make something to eat. Eddie was having none of it, indicating for her to pass him his dressing gown. She obeyed. Wrapping the green robe around him, she left the room.

The apartment needed a good overhaul. There were a few pots lying around, the odd plate still bore left over food. Angel tidied up. Finishing as Eddie emerged from the bedroom. The transformation remarkable. Washed and dressed, she watched in admiration as he crossed to the settee. He was a survivor and had no intention of giving up without a fight.

Cancer would not defeat him. Yes, he felt ill on some days, well most days. He had lost a lot of weight from his already slim body, but he was coping. The thought of leaving his daughter alone pushing him on with each fresh day.

When he saw the daughter of old, he loved her more than words could describe. The cold, calculating Angel he despaired about. 'I know I've caused you pain dad. Done things you don't understand but I love you. I meant it when I said it all over now.' The sudden statement from his daughter caught him off guard.

He ignored the subject of murder. More out of a selfish need to talk to the Angel of the moment than anything else. 'I've had further tests to determine how much of my liver is damaged. Maybe I'm in time to still have surgery. ' A sad smile crept over Angel's lips. She had only to look at the yellowing of his skin to know surgery would not help.

'I told you I was going away for a few weeks. The book tour, remember? Why don't you come with me? Get some quality time together.' Sorely tempted. It would give him thinking time away from Castleton. With medication, it could work. No alcohol, regular exercise, it could perfect. It could be the last time he could share real time with her daughter.

The thought of reminiscing, happy memories, times with Carrie and Angel. Laughing again. To see his daughter doing her readings to adoring audiences. The thought overjoyed him. It would be magical. Carrie would have jumped at such a chance had she been given the chance.

TORMENTED

'How about it, dad? It will be just you, me and mum. She will be with us in our memories.' If only he could be sure that his health would hold out. Not taking up his daughter's offer could be worse. Wait too long. He could be dead, or Angel would be in prison, caught for her crimes.

'I need to speak to Dr Morton first, see what he thinks. But you know, Angel, I think it's a marvellous idea. It really appeals.' Both aware that this would be a onetime opportunity only. 'You get onto the doc; I'll make the arrangements.' Excited, she skipped out of the apartment.

Warm sun shone down on her as she crossed the park. Two policemen were talking to the dealers, idling around their adopted bench. A common sight since the murder. She thought no more of it. Smiled, waved and strolled on.

There was a sense of safety in the Town now. The high visibility of officers plodding the narrow streets had reduced general crime. Castleton had been a happier place in recent weeks. Fewer drunks dawdling at night.

Keen to understand as much as she could about her father's condition, Angel tapped the word Sorofenib into her keypad. 'Sorofenib belongs to a class of medicines called kinases. Kinases are one of the types of chemicals that control the growth of cells and blood vessels. By blocking the effects of these chemicals, Sorafenib may help to slow the growth of cancer.'

Angel read and re-read. Her forehead creased in deep crevices as she digested the information. The side effects were many. Nausea, weight loss, bleeding, pain, on and on. What her father was going through was more than she could ever imagine. Still, he put her first. Guilt overwhelmed her. She had to make their last journey special.

She had avenged her mother; it was done. Deep down she knew he was glad. In a world of her own now, she saw them sitting together on the train. Her mother smiling at them, her father gripping her hand. Something he had always done when she was a child.

With Bobby Brooks close to taking her in for questioning, she had no time to waste. The last journey she and her father would take together must be sorted. Arrangements made; bags packed. The finest hotels, best food. He would have everything he needed.

She would introduce him as her father, that would please him. She would say it was him who had inspired her to write. He would glow with pride. His face would fill with emotion as he listened to her read. For the first time in weeks, Angel felt a sense of satisfaction.

A4 pad in hand, she planned. That night, she lay her head on her pillow feeling a sense of achievement.

TORMENTED

Content, she drifted into sleep. She was beside her mother; they were in the park. Dressed identically. They could be mistaken for twins. Long red hair, green eyes, strappy heels. Red dress, white shawls. Life was satisfying.

The colours were brighter than Angel had ever seen and impossible to describe. No such colours existed in her world. The park was different, the space vast. The heat warmed her skin; she felt totally loved. Her mother's smile unlike any she had seen before. This is where she wanted to stay forever. It wasn't to be.

In an instance, the scene had changed. Now lying on the floor, blood streaming from her head. Her mother gone, in her place a group of men. Laughing, shouting. Kicking at her, jabbing her flesh. Vulnerable, alone. Struggling to move, get up. Scream out but her voice silent. Everything around her sinister, dark, cold. Shapes moving, stamping on her, jeering. Agonising pain filling her body. Unable to defend herself.

Sweat poured from her forehead as she sat up with a start. She hated these dreams but couldn't stop them. She had been crying. It was the same vision replayed over and over during her sleeping hours. Visions she couldn't control and hated. Her longing to wake up refreshed, feel good again, haunted her.

Instead, her senses were always dulled. She was never totally alert. She always felt disturbed upon waking. The only times she felt alert were sickening to her. Made her question her motives. Did she commit the crimes to revenge her mother or because of the feeling of gratification it gave her? It was an answer she didn't want to know.

The train left the station on time. Angel had booked first-class tickets. Breakfast was served on china plates. Little white napkins were wrapped around silver cutlery. It was joyous to her. She was like a gleeful child. Eddie approved. She rattled on about the comfort of the seats, the space between them. Anything and nothing of importance.

It reminded him of his visits back to Castleton when he worked in the big City. Carrie used to love first class travel. Gave her a few airs and graces. A true lady, Eddie had smiled at the way she sipped her coffee, her little finger stuck up in the air. Small sips, always silent. Carrie couldn't stand noisy eaters. A clear sign of a bad upbringing, she used to remark.

Kings Cross was a hive of activity. The buzz of a capital city. A place of hello's, goodbyes and the unknown. A place of mixed emotions, great happiness for some, deep loneliness for others. Irrespective of which it was an experience not forgotten.

Hustling her father through the gate, towards the taxi rank, they were soon pulling up outside of the Stafford Hotel. A small but luxurious hotel with large suites.

TORMENTED

Perfect for a two-week stay. Accessible to Hyde Park and the prime shopping areas.

It had been a while since Angel had stayed here, but she knew the hotel well. Here there were no nosy staff to disturb them. The suite she had booked, with its two on-suite bedrooms and a view over the park to die for, got a further nod of approval from her father.

Satisfied that it was an acceptable place for him to be, she had also made sure that a doctor's surgery was in the vicinity, although hoped they would have no need of it.

For the next two weeks Castleton and what awaited them upon their return would be forgotten about. They would concentrate all efforts on Angel's career. School visits, publisher meetings. All black thoughts would remain well hidden. The fortnight would be about the two of them only.

The classroom was cosy, children sat in a circle. A plump, officious looking teacher introduced Angel. She flipped the book open prior to acknowledging the wide-eyed group; the reading began. Eager faces listened intently. Eyes sparkled in anticipation.

'That is why you must always do good, always your best and remember to love your parents.'

Applause drowned out the thankyous. Eddie observed the surreal scene. His thoughts cast back to the faces of the victim's families he had interviewed. How could the woman stood before him, entertaining enthralled youngsters, kill in cold blood? Much as he wanted, he couldn't rid himself of his thoughts. Who was this person? This kind-hearted soul, delighting in the joy of her small audience?

Over a sumptuous meal he praised his daughter's artistic abilities. They conversed as if the situation was normal. Discussed her work, the tour. What they would be see, where they would go. The conversation light-hearted. Angel enthused how her latest book was being printed in various languages. The result, an overseas tour. Eddie listened, his face beaming. His heart heavy. He knew there was no reality in her words.

His daughter would be behind bars long before any overseas tour began. He wouldn't be at her trial. No one would be there to support her. He wouldn't be able to hang on that long and he knew it. Day by day he was getting weaker. The best he could hope for is that they would find her insane.

It was important to Eddie that he talk to Bobby, explain his daughter's mental state. Make him understand that she had a dual personality. Plead with him, make sure he looked after her. She had filled his prayers night and day. He prayed over and over for leniency. He would call in every favour owing to him to give her the best chance of survival.

'A bottle of your best Chablis please.' Eddie snapped back to their current situation. Angel smiling at him, showing him a good time. She seemed oblivious to the reckoning he knew was to come. 'You'll like this dad, it's a good wine.' Eddie preferred a pint but knew to order one would embarrass his daughter.

To him, wine was wine, but to his daughter it was important that it tasted excellent, the best. She was going to substantial lengths to make this time special for them both and he knew it. He gulped a mouthful of the nectar, swilled it around, pretending to be knowledgeable, and commented how light it was.

He couldn't help wondering, would she go to such lengths if it weren't because he was on death row? Tonight, he'd make a real attempt to dismiss his reservations and embrace the uniqueness of the occasion.

In-between school and publisher visits, Angel had arranged museum visits, theatre treats and several other outings she thought her father would enjoy, Madame Tussauds one of them. Walking around the general section was tiring Eddie at the pace his daughter set. There were times he would have enjoyed staying in the comfort of his hotel suite, resting.

At other times, he longed for an in-depth conversation with Angel. Talk about her future, what it would mean for her should they convict her. Her excitement at visiting the horror chamber put paid to any thoughts he had of resting or settling into a sensible conversation.

There was no hurrying through this section. One by one, Angel studied the exhibits. Joyfully, remarking at the crimes that had been committed. Discussing their methods as if comparing. Eddie watched in silence as his daughter relished the scenes. Her eyes cold and icy. 'Do you think I could get into a place like this dad?' 'What?' He was shocked. 'Do you realise how much suffering you have caused to innocent people? Are you at all aware of the serious, of the trouble you are in?'

For an instance, he thought he saw a sign of remorse. He was wrong. Angel showed only contempt for her father's words. She continued her examination of the waxworks, paying no heed to the conversation. Forgotten as if it never existed.

The rest of the two weeks continued without further events. The relationship between them uneasy. Conversation stunted. Angel continued the harsh schedule she had set herself whilst Eddie found some rest time he desperately needed.

Time to study his next actions. He was a dying man, not long left. Should he try to protect his daughter? What if he took the blame, would he get away with it?

Could he do such a thing? Sully his reputation, would it matter now? So many questions. He hoped, beyond hope, he would find answers before they returned to Castleton.

On the journey home, Eddie felt sick, spending most of his time in the bathroom. Angel sat sipping champagne, tapping away at her Nexus tablet. It would please Eddie to get home. He had made important decisions and needed to act.

Used to travel and indifferent to where it took her, home had no real meaning for her anymore. Eddie thanked her for the special time that they had spent together. Her eyes filled with water. She squeezed his frail hand. 'It's not going to be long Angel.' 'I know dad.' For a brief minute, their eyes met, both resigned to their fates.

Damage Limitation

Overwhelmed with sadness at the sight of his friend, Bobby Brooks beckoned Eddie into his office. It had only been two weeks since they last spoke. There was a marked deterioration. Eddie's eyes were bloodshot. A yellow pallor covered the skin stretched tight across his gaunt face. The weight loss was dramatic. In a slow and awkward gait, he moved towards the chair. The pain he was in etched on his face.

Bobby rushed to pull the chair out. He immediately ordered coffee for his friend. With genuine concern for the reporter who had helped him solve so many crimes, he gave orders they were not to be disturbed. Eddie struggled to get his breath back. His decision to walk up the 20 steps to the second floor had been a mistake.

'We need to talk Bob.' The Chief Constable nodded, waiting for Eddie to continue. Where to start was a problem. So much had to be said. So much needed to be agreed. Eddie had to be sure that his daughter would be taken care of. He couldn't see her thrown into some jail and the key tossed away. He had to make Bobby recognise that his daughter was ill. Get her the tests needed to prove that she was mentally unstable.

'I haven't got long to go, Bob. I'm dying from liver cancer.' Bobby opened his mouth as if to speak, but no words came out. Eddie continued to explain his condition and diagnosis. 'I'm refusing chemo, treatments would just prolong the inevitable. I can't put Angel through that. She had suffered enough in her life Bob. I don't know how much time I have to go, but I have to know Angel will be okay.'

Bobby Brooks didn't know how to answer. What was the man he had known since a boy about to ask him? Would it compromise his post and his job?' He felt sick inside. How could he tell a dying man that he couldn't and wouldn't break the law? His fears subsided as Eddie spoke, his breathing erratic. 'There's a lot to do. I must plan my funeral and I want you to help me do it, Bobby. I can't ask Angel; she has a lot of problems of her own. 'My only request is that you make sure she leads the service.'

He had to make Bobby realise how important his last wish was to him and to Angel. 'You stood by me Bob, even when I was heavy on the drink. I know you put a beat man to watch I got home. Thank you, but I need one more favour, just one more.'

Apprehension surmounted; Bob eyed his friend. 'I'll do what I can buddy but don't ask me to break the law. I can't do that, even for you.

The sincerity in the lawman's voice echoed through the words. They had been friends, allies and more for many years. The respect they held for each other, strong. Eddie smiled and pulled a crumpled piece of paper from his pocket.

He tossed the paper onto the table.' I know Bob; you don't have to tell me that. We have to talk about Angel though, off the record, for old friendships.' Without commenting further, Bobby Brooks unfolded the scrimped-up paper and smoothed it out. He read the list of instructions.

Songs, hymns, church reception guests, sayings. It covered everything needed to arrange and conduct a funeral. Bob nodded, folded the sheet and shoved it into his inside pocket. 'It will do done buddy. To the letter.'

Next, Eddie drew an envelope from inside his jacket. It was marked private. 'I need you to read this after my death. It's my last will and testament. Promise me that's when you will open it.' Eddie's hand trembled as he pushed the letter across.

'Angel isn't well Bob; I think she's mentally unstable. What do I do, I don't know anymore? I need to protect her. Help her. I was not always there for her as a child.

I must be there for her now, but how? I'm as much to blame as her for anything she may have done. Her mother's death, the way of it. It affected her a lot. Was I so blind I couldn't see how much she was suffering? Where was I, I should have? I failed her. So, hooked up in my shit and self-pity. I can't run out of time, Bob. I just can't.'

His head in his hands, Eddie broke down, sobbing like a lost soul. Bob felt his pain. He handed him a box of tissues and placed a solid arm around his shoulder. Pulling his chair with his free hand, he sat facing his old friend. Their knees almost touching. The aged, tired looking policeman spoke quietly as Eddie listened. They would need to open with each other, trust each other more than ever before.

'Look, Angel isn't a suspect yet. Just a person of interest to us. Let's get lunch, talk. You know I can't do that here.' The two left the office, Bob striding in front, Eddie shuffling behind him.

As an investigative reporter dealing with crime and its consequences, Eddie knew all aspects of the criminal system. He had studied long and hard during his early days. Even sitting exams in criminology. Several times Eddie had contemplated becoming a criminologist but never taken it forward. He also knew there was no such thing as 'off the record' he used the term so many times but this time he had to put any faith he had in Bobby Brooks.

A quick word to an officer on the way out. He turned, saw his friend struggling and supported him as they descended the stairs. Eddie's eyes were red, he coughed. Stopping to let him catch his breath, Bob squeezed his hand.

'Taxi.' Bob waved his hand up and down. A cab pulled up at the curb edge. Eddie tried to protest he didn't need a cab but was beyond arguing. Slumping onto the seat, he sat back. Bobby directed the driver to his friend's apartment block.

'I don't know where the fuck to start Bob. I'm so lost with this.' Angel was different, she had always been different. Intelligent, studious. Preferring to study than go out with friends. There had been few boyfriends that Eddie could remember. None ever lasted long, none introduced or invited home.

Angel spoke little of her thoughts, keeping herself to herself. Protective of her privacy. School reports described her as a loner, preferring her own company to that of her peers. A disciplined student who applied herself well to her work. It wasn't surprising that she gained good grades before going onto university to study creative writing. There was never any doubt she would be successful in her chosen career.

To all intents and purposes, Angel Boyle was the ideal daughter. Never bringing trouble home. Very self-sufficient and confident in all she did. In recent weeks

Eddie realised, however, just how little he knew of his daughter. Who her friends were, did she have any friends? He had met none of them. Did she have interests other than writing? He had no idea. Did Carrie know her better?

She was closer to Carrie, and that stuck in his throat. Ashamed, he couldn't remember taking the time to get to know his daughter. Too involved with his own life. He had never let her in.

'This is off the record isn't it? We're talking as friends?' Bob nodded an affirmative. 'I think she may know something about the killings. I don't want to think it, but I do. I love her Bob; I can't see her locked up for the rest of her life. She needs help and its breaking me in two knowing I won't be here to help her. I need you to promise me you will.' Eddie Boyle's voice filled with desperation.

He knew Bobby well enough to know he was putting two and two together and that soon all fingers would point to Angel. Bob Brooks already knew of her involvement. His eyes couldn't hide it from Eddie. It was just a matter of time and solidifying the proof needed.

In the past they had sat and discussed many cases, many facts and leads. Eddie using his own polished investigative skills to assist Bobby bring the cases to an early close. It was clear to both men; they had avoided talking about the murders, something they would normally have done. Bob knew there had to be a reason. Bob chose to put it down to Eddie's health.

The two men understood each other. A look had always said a hundred words when working a case together. 'I'll do all I can Eddie, but you need to tell me all that you know now. This must end. I have several forces breathing down my neck. Officers from all over the region sitting in my backyard. Cameras and reporters all over town stirring up any shit they can find. If you can help me bring this to a close Eddie, I need you to do it.'

The pressure that came with unsolved murders was well known to Eddie. The long nights debating over the facts, pondering the unknowns. Bob would have had little sleep or peace. It was taking its toll on him; it was written all over his face. He didn't need to be told what the right thing was to do but his heart was ripping in two between his duty as a moral citizen and his loyalty to his own kin.

TORMENTED

A Raw Dilemma

All Eddie wanted to do was disappear. Become someone else. His bones ached; his head pounded. His confusion becoming stronger with each thought. He looked at Bob, his eyes glazed over. How far should he go in his confession to him?

'The death of Carrie affected her Bob, more than you could ever know. I didn't know just how crushed she was. She is so good at hiding her feelings. Angel's hard to read Bob but she thinks so deeply. Things disturb her, her dreams haunt her. The books she writes are at odds with what's in her mind. Her sense of justice distorted, but it's hers. She believes it.'

'What are you trying to tell me Eddie?' Bobby Brooks was in no mood for long drawn out games. He was desperate to get things back to normal. The tension at the station, the constant news coverage. Media down his neck. He was too old for all of this but wouldn't let up until he solved the murders that had turned his much-loved Castleton upside down.

Oblivious to anything but the pain he was feeling, Eddie continued his soliloquy. 'I have tried to shield her, all her life, I have done my best to protect her from the terrors of this world but, I failed to protect her from herself. She's bright, clever. Intelligent, naturally so, Bob. She's done so well.' Eddie's voice rose and fell as he sang his daughters praises.

'Have you seen her apartment? It is beautiful. Grand furniture, all you would want for your daughter and more. I've never been so scared, Bob. That's the truth of it. She'll be on her own. Lost no one to guard her. It kills me. It's hopeless, I'm hopeless, for once I can't do anything about it and it's killing me inside.'

Bob felt his pain. 'She used to say that when she was famous, she would buy an island, build a sizeable house where we could all be together. Her, Carrie and me. An idyllic place just for us.' A wry smile crept across Eddie's face. The thought a million miles away. Far out of reach.

'The only way we'll be together now is when we all meet on the other side. I'd feel easier if I thought Carrie and me would still look out for her. I wish my beliefs were deeper. More solid. They're not Bob. They're not.'

TORMENTED

Eddie was now speaking rapidly, talking. His breath, quick, shallow. Racing for time to get his message across. 'I can't work this one out. Can't solve it, the solution is beyond my control, Bob. I need help. Actual help. I'm lost in a pool with no way out.'

Angel would have been unforgiving had she known that her father was pouring out his thoughts to Bobby Brooks. She knew he was carrying a deep sadness. A sense of loss that she was not helping. Didn't she lay awake at nights wondering what it would be like to know you only had weeks left to live? How would she feel if she only had a brief time left on this Earth? Pity for her father ran amok within her. His deterioration had been so rapid. Changes were now daily. Each one worse than the last.

What her next steps were to be, she did not understand. Once he was gone, what then? What was left for her? Give herself up or move, build a new life? Fearful of being alone, incarcerated with no one to write to, no one to visit, scared the shit out of her. She appeared, but she knew that she wasn't as brave or as capable as she tried hard to make others believe.

Sometimes she felt nothing at all. Times when she saw her life as pointless. Other occasions she would look at her world and thank God for what she had. Her achievements were many, especially her literary ones. It was during those times she felt most at peace.

Contented with the World. Sadly, they were few and far between.

Now, closer to her father than ever before, she still harboured confusion. How much she loved him. He was never there for her as a child. Never went to school plays, helped her with homework. Listened to her read. Hugged her when she got hurt. He limited the time he gave her to the point of resentment.

It had been her mother who had done all the childhood things with her. Dressed up with her, baked with her. Combed her hair, loved her. Nursed her when ill. Waited with her for her father to come home, only for him to call at the Moon first. Returning past her bedtime.

The effect of Eddie's desperation on Bobby Brooks was clear. He felt he was in an almost impossible situation. His friend was suffering, he wanted more than anything to help, but how? Angel had not been accused of anything outright. No one could force her to have a test, only appeal to her sense of right and wrong. Yet here was the finest reporter he knew, suggesting she was involved.

If she was, as Eddie was telling him, unbalanced. A plea of insanity would commit her to life in an institution. How she would cope with that he had no idea? She would at least get treatment. Would prison be better with its educational programmes, leaving her free to continue to write and publish? Was he looking too far ahead? Was she capable of killing without any remorse? He had to know.

'Are you trying to say that Angel has responsibility for these murders, Eddie?'

'EDDIE.' Bobby rushed across to the settee where Eddie had slumped forward, head in hands, gasping for breath. Without another word, he rang 999.

Angel was waiting at the hospital when the ambulance arrived. She cast a quick glance towards Bobby Brooks as she rushed to the trolley on which her father lay. A team of doctors were rushing around, they had attached wires and lines to him. Machines were bleeping.

In silence, she sat listening to the rhythm of his shallow heartbeat, taking in the bleep that emitted with each laboured breath. The figure in the bed didn't look like her father. In his place lay an ashen faced, vulnerable, old man with sallow cheeks. His body only a skeleton.

Startled by a firm hand touching her shoulder, she jumped. Turned and saw the white coat of a young doctor. Strong and handsome, in other circumstances she may even have been attracted to him. All she thought now was that he was too young to be caring for her terminally ill father.

'Miss Boyle, can we speak in private?' Puzzling why Bobby Brooks had arrived at A&E with her father, she noted how he had now moved to lean over her father, the concern on his face clear. Was he waiting for him to die to arrest her? Why else was he there? It troubled her.

'Miss Boyle, did you hear me? Can we step into another room? Your father is extremely ill. Is there anyone else you would like us to contact to be here with you? Angel didn't respond. Bobby Brooks had walked into the corridor and was now on his mobile. 'Miss Boyle?' Angel didn't respond, instead she moved to her father's bedside. She didn't want to hear what she already knew. The reality too much for her.

Except for two nurses sitting outside of the emergency room, the corridor was deserted. Bobby Brooks had long since gone home. It was now nearing midnight. A tired Angel wanted to sleep but the fear of losing her father as she slept, kept her awake.

Eddie had drifted in and out of consciousness since his arrival, but his heart remained at a steady beat. That gave her some reassurance. She had shared a lot with him in the past few weeks and longed for more time. The hours passed. Her father remained stable. Unable to fight any longer, her eyes closed. The emotion of the day had taken its toll. Unwillingly, she fell asleep on the small cot reserved for visitors.

Woken to a dawn chorus, Angel stretched, becoming aware the bleeping had stopped. Her heart missed a beat. She sprang to her father's bedside. 'Morning love.' His voice was almost chirpy. Angel was angry. She didn't like to show such reactions. Eddie smiled. 'I scared you love, sorry.' 'I thought I'd lost you.' Her voice cracked with emotion.

Wire free, Eddie was sitting up in bed, a cup of tea by his side. 'What happened, dad? Did you phone the police before me? Unsure what to say, he shrugged his shoulders. Relieved when the nurse came striding into the room. 'Remember, you must not miss your tablets again. They are for a reason Mr Boyle.' Full of apologies all Eddie cared about was going home.

'Get me out of here Angel, if I'm going to die it's going to be in my home.' Staring hard, her words firm and assertive. 'No dad, I'll only consent to you coming out if you come to mine. I can look after you there. I won't allow them to send you home.' Caught by surprise, Eddie nodded. There was nothing he would like more than to end his days in his daughter's care.

Three days later Eddie was settled in Angel's apartment. Weak but pain free. The fentanyl patch was an effective control and he could put up with the constipation and sickness to be near his daughter. The codeine top-up he tried to avoid taking but knew he had them available should he need them.

It was a strange situation, one that Angel had never envisaged but was weirdly comforting to her. How long it would last was unknown. What she would do when the end came, unclear. It was important now that she remained in control. Supervised her father's medication and kept him as stable as possible.

Today was another day. If her father were well enough, she would take him to lunch. Have a walk through the park, around the town centre. Things she recalled doing as a family. 'How do you feel dad?' Angel hoped the response would be positive. It was.

Try as he might, Eddie could manage no more than a few paces before stopping for breath. 'I'm sorry Angel, I just can't keep up with you.' It didn't matter to her. It could take all day. What else was there to do, sit and watch him slowly pass away?

The coffee shop was empty. A grateful Eddie plonked down near the window. The view over the square was a welcome sight. People carry on about their everyday lives. Not knowing how short their time could be. If Eddie was honest, the thought of his own death frightened him. Would he be gasping for breath? Die in his bed, in his sleep? How would Angel react to finding him? Perhaps he should have stayed in hospital, asked to go to a hospice?

'Penny for em dad.' 'They're not worth that much love.' Angel laughed. The coffee was excellent. The window seat even better. Across the street from the café, high above the sidewalk, lived the market clock. A meeting place for young and old alike. Beneath it, the entrance to the market. Another of the Victorian buildings that made up the architecture of Castleton.

A faraway look in her father's eyes told Angel he was thinking about her mother. The times they had met under the clock. 'Do you ever think what it would have been like without that night dad?' 'All the time Angel. The way it happened. How I let her down.' Silence fell on father and daughter as they focused their attention on the bustling figures ambling their time away. Chatting, smiling, unaware of the future.

Several youngsters were playing in the park. A young couple sat in the bandstand kissing, oblivious to the two individuals passing by. Angel and Eddie looked at each other and giggled. 'Young love, so innocent and free.'

Most of the park benches were covered in graffiti. Names of occupants with nothing better to do than destroy. Eddie welcomed the rest, watching amused as Angel took out the swiss army knife, her father had given her for protection. With precision she carved the initials EB, CB and AB into the wood. Next, she etched a heart shape around the letters. 'Always remembered now, dad.'

'Need to get back. Medication time, dad.' Angel held out her arm for her father to hold. 'I've enjoyed today. It's given me time to think. Bobby will take care of it, Angel. Everything will be fine. You don't have to be concerned any more. You do know I love you, don't you?' Angel wasn't worried in the least, she was realistic enough to know her life was about to change again. It would be a matter of weeks at the most.

Plans were already in hand. Seeing Bobby Brooks at the hospital had pushed her forward. How much her father had shared with him she didn't know, but she knew what she had to do when the unavoidable happened. Angel would board a flight to LA. Staying at the little hideaway she had once rented before. Here she knew she could write under a pen name and live in the isolation she craved. Castleton, its imagery, the nightmares, all behind her.

Her father would understand her decision not to attend his funeral. Would want her to start again, leave the past behind. He'd be the first to tell her to block it out. Lead her own life. Risking being charged for murder would serve nothing. If she disappeared, no one could charge her with anything. In time the murders would go cold. Justice carried out. Her mother revenged. Her father back with her mother, at peace.

'Drink up before it's cold.' 'It's wine, dad. It is cold. 'They laughed. Angel pushed a DVD into the machine and sat back to watch 'Lawrence of Arabia' her father's favourite film. Eddie took his daughter's hand and held it. Together they fell asleep. The two empty pill bottles hidden behind the cushion his body rested upon.

TORMENTED

The decision made by Eddie had been the hardest he had ever made. Deep down, he knew Angel wouldn't survive prison alone. An asylum would be worse. He had wrestled long and hard with his conscience. Men had died because of his own daughter's twisted view of justice. He couldn't ignore it. He had to report it.

Bob may not understand his decision or agree with it, but Eddie knew his friend wouldn't judge him. He would carry out his funeral wishes to the letter. A friend he could rely on to the very end.

The message on Bobby Brooks answer machine made little sense. 'It's time to come to Angel's place old friend. I'll leave the door unlocked.' Eddie's voice cracked as he spoke. It was clear something was wrong. The feeling in the pit of the police officer's stomach confirmed it.

What met Bobby Brooks made his blood run cold. It was quiet in the apartment. A sweet vanilla odour hung in the air. Empty wine glasses sat on a coffee table, one overturned. A burnt down candle, it's wick still smoking. In Eddie's hand an envelope. Scribbled on the front '**For the attention of Inspector Brooks.'**

Rooted to the spot, Bobby Brooks cast a teary eye around the apartment. Nothing appeared to be out of place. It could have been a cosy family scene in any home in the country. Father and daughter sat together, enjoying a drink. It wasn't. The difference, both were deceased.

Eyes closed; the experienced police inspector wept. His heart ached for the friend he saw as a brother. For a family destroyed by a series of events no one had foreseen or being able to prevent.

In a daze, he moved towards the bodies. Careful not to touch anything on the table, he pressed two fingers on the neck of his friend. There was no pulse. He repeated the action on Angel; the result was the same. He flinched at the warmth of their skin. It was clear they had not been deceased long. He saw now signs of rigor mortis. The look on their faces was peaceful. A look he hadn't seen on his friend's face for a long time.

TORMENTED

The Letter

It would take a while before forensics arrived and they could move the corpses. Bobby would have to wait until they had finished. It was the last thing he wanted to do, but he had limited options.

Stood in silence, he collected his thoughts. At what point, if any, had they agreed to commit suicide? Eddie he could understand, he had only days to live, but Angel. Had she been so mad that she preferred to die before face jail? Was it a joint suicide or something else?

It was time to read the letter, now photographed, dusted for prints and tucked in his pocket, aching to be opened. Here was not the place.

Back in his office, Bobby Brooks hung a **DO NOT DISTURB** notice on his door. Drew the blinds and sat down. For a long while, he stared into space. Part of him needing to read the letter, now sitting on the desk before him. Part of him dreading its contents.

He pondered life. Memories of drunken, youthful nights spend in the Moon. The years he had tried to persuade Eddie to become a copper. Reading at the wedding of him and Carrie. Holding Angel as a baby. Fun days, happy times. Making blood pacts as kids. All in the past now, destroyed by a single event capable of turning lives around so rapidly, there seemed to have been nothing before it.

Why hadn't they been able to find the culprits? Would any of this happened if they had? Did he try hard enough? Could more enquiries have been made? All unknown's but all relevant. Was he even a good copper anymore? He had been once. Perhaps now he should retire. Leave it to the youngsters with their new ways.

Several minutes passed, then, in slow motion, he opened the envelope, unfolded several types written pages and began to read.

For the attention of Detective Inspector Robert Brooks.

Where do I start, old friend? What brought me to this? I have tried to recompense myself with the events of the last few years but without success. I am paying for something, what escapes me. Am I such a bad person that I have deserved this?

TORMENTED

I must start with the night of the attack. I lied Bob, lied to cover up my guilt. Said that I didn't see Carrie leave. Yes, I did, but was just too selfish to leave with her. Winning the challenge cup was more important to me, but the truth is, the game had already finished. I could have followed her. I didn't. I wanted to stay and celebrate my pathetic victory. I have never forgiven myself for that.

Carrie was totally innocent. Not a bad bone in her body. What happened to her is beyond my understanding. The aftermath worse still. My wife died that night, out on the street in a filthy back alley. The person who came back to me was no more than an empty shell. Night after night she woke screaming, kicking out. Re-living her terrors. She had no life. She was locked away in her own thoughts. Do you know what it's like for someone to beg you to release them from their torment? Over and over she pleaded with me to end her suffering. Then I gave in to her.

I told you I was out shopping when she committed suicide. Another lie. I was with her throughout. The hook was fixed by me, not her. She was too weak even to tie the knot; I did it for her. Watched as she swallowed the tablets. Handfuls she took. Waited until she was groggy then helped her put the noose around her neck, and I walked away. I heard the snap when she fell to the ground. Saw her contorted face.

I wanted to end it myself that day. Be with her. Only my own cowardice stopped me. Carrie was the strongest of us. Angel takes after her.

I can never justify what I did. I haven't been able to live with myself. Liver cancer is my payback. It's the least I deserve. The loneliness I've felt unbearable. Then Angel started to visit me. What that meant, I cannot tell you. You couldn't understand Bob.

Then the murders started. For the first time in a long time, Angel took an interest in who I spoke to and what you and I knew about the killings. My instinct told me that the interest was abnormal, but I pushed it aside. Only when I read the description of the woman, you released, did I question her motives.

I knew the clothing description was almost identical to the clothing Carrie wore when attacked. I made myself think it was a coincidence. After forensics had finished, I got her clothes back. I knew no one would have remembered what Carrie wore that night or linked the two. I should have come clean, but I couldn't lay suspicion on Angel. I had to protect her; she was all I had left. There was no proof to say it involved her. I couldn't make accusations against my kin without hard facts.

The last few months are the closest I have been with my daughter. Being able to talk to her, share with her, and feel useful in her life. Well, it made me feel good

Bob. I know that's not enough, but it's all I have to offer. My mind fought to put aside the victims' families and their suffering. I know now, writing this, I could have saved at least one of them. I regret not offering coming forward. It has torn me apart.

More than anything, my heart bleeds for Angel. The way she turned hot and cold. The look she had when talking about the cases. A coldness I have never encountered before. Her belief she was talking to her mother. I recognised it distorted her reality. Admitting my daughter was mad was more than I could bear.

You need to know that we have all suffered. Angel may have committed horrendous crimes but believed she was revenging her mother. In her mind, the men she killed were the same culprits who had savagely assaulted Carrie. She was convinced that they deserved it.

I must tell you she wouldn't have continued. She believed Carrie had told her it was over. Angel convinced herself that Carrie was guiding her actions and was asking her to avenge her death.

She did wrong, but I couldn't stand by and watch her go to prison. We belong together, we always belonged together. I know you can't understand. You would, had you lived through the pain we have lived through.

I'm here now, writing this. Angel has fallen asleep. She doesn't understand that I'm taking her with me. No idea that I ground tablets into her drink. She was in no pain; I know it's what she wanted.

I've waited until she's stopped breathing to take my tablets. I must be sure I haven't made any mistakes. The atmosphere is almost serene. We've watched a film together. I've held her hand. Now there's a silence I can't describe.

I'm feeling drowsy now, I'm shaking Bob, I admit I'm feeling scared but now it's too late. It's time to go. Forgive me for everything, Bob. I didn't have the proof I needed to share any information with you before. No definite proof. Not until we walked through the park yesterday and Angel stopped to carve our initials on the old oak tree.

Then it hit me, the childhood game we played. She would change letters for numbers, her secret code. 32, it made sense. The numbers represent the letters CB, Carrie Boyle, they are her initials.

I need to finish now; I'm finding it hard to focus and hold the pen. Remember us for the good times, rather than the bad. This is the only way forward. Give us a good send off, pal.

CASE CLOSED
EDDIE BOYLE

About the Author

Patricia A Sutcliffe is a retired university lecturer and experienced human behaviourist with a passion for writing. Her first achievement as a writer came when she took first place in a national school competition at 10 years of age. Since then she has had poetry published and several articles on human development.

Her enthusiasm for Crime novels came from her study of forensic criminology. **'Tormented'** is the accumulation of her many years of writing and is her first crime genre novel.

Her interests are wide ranging from writing to water colour painting to teaching chess as a registered coach. She established the first Junior Chess Club in the town where she lives. To becoming a Town Mayor, counsellor and consultant.

Printed in Poland
by Amazon Fulfillment
Poland Sp. z o.o., Wrocław